TOTO

THE WIZARD OF OZ

as told by the dog

To Anoushka ~ M.M.

To Caroline ~ E.C.C.

michael morpurgo

TOTO

THE WIZARD OF OZ

as told by the dog

Illustrated by Emma Chichester Clark

HarperCollins *Children's Books*

CONTENTS

PROLOGUE

———◆———

I Was There…

*T*hat was how Papa Toto always began his story: *"I was there." There were seven of us puppies, and that's a lot, and I was the littlest. Papa Toto always called me Tiny Toto. Whenever Mama lay down in the basket to feed us, my brothers and sisters just trampled all over me to get to her first. Mama hardly noticed me, I was so small, but Papa Toto did. He always saw to it there was a proper place for me, and when the others pushed me off, he'd nose them away to make room for*

me. Without Papa Toto I guess I wouldn't ever have had enough milk, would probably never have lived to grow up at all and tell the tale.

Papa Toto's tale was the best part of every day for me. Papa Toto would wait till Mama had climbed out of the basket and gone out of the house with all the people folk. Like Dorothy, who Papa Toto loved almost as much as he loved me. And that wasn't just because I was the littlest and the best-looking but because I was the only one who was always still awake at the end of his story. We didn't see too much of him during the day. He was out most of the day on the farm working alongside Dorothy and Uncle Henry and Aunt Em, ploughing and sowing. Of course, Papa Toto didn't do all the chores himself – that was people folk's work – but he did drive the cows, keep an eye out for snakes and wolves and the like, and chase rabbits and rats and mice whenever and wherever he found them.

And on the lazy hot days he'd just hang around, making sure Dorothy didn't come to harm. "It's what I'm for," he'd tell us. "Wherever she goes, I go. But now you littl'uns are around, Dorothy says I got to look after you from time to time, give your mama a break from you. But I don't want none of your wriggling and clambering and tumbling out like you do, and no chewing on my tail. No piddling in the basket, y'hear. Dorothy don't like it when you piddle on the floor neither. And don't go pestering me for food, cos you ain't going to get none – I've told you time and again that's what your mama does, not me. You just lie still and go to sleep."

But lying still only ever happened when we were all fast asleep, and Papa Toto had his own special way of getting us to do that. He'd be telling us one of his stories, and, sure enough, pretty soon all the wriggling and clambering and the tumbling stopped, and we'd all be lying there still and listening, all seven of us. And then, one by one they'd all drop off to sleep and in the end I'd often be the only one left awake, because I always wanted to hear what happened in the end. The way I saw it, there wasn't much point in listening to the beginning of the story if you didn't hear how it finished. Of course, I knew what happened in the end – we had all heard Papa Toto's stories often enough. But it was the way he told them that kept me awake, kept me listening, like he was there inside the story and I was right there with him.

Even so, I've got to say – but don't you go telling him now – I did drop off during some of his tales. But there was one story I stayed awake to hear from beginning to end, the one about the Wizard of Oz, the one he always began with: "I was there." Papa Toto especially loved telling that story, and we loved hearing it. The way he told it you just had to believe every last word of it. Of course, I never believed it afterwards. But I wanted to. It was funny and frightening, and sad and silly, and weird and wonderful, and so amazing and exciting that I never wanted to go to sleep, however warm and snug and full up with milk I was. That was Papa Toto's best tale, the one I longed for, the one I never fell asleep in. He'd climb into our basket in the corner of the room, turn round and round, and then lie down carefully, trying not to squash any of us, but he always did, and this time it was me.

"Sorry, Tiny Toto," he said, nudging me gently with his cold, cold nose. He waited until all the squealing and squeaking had stopped, till we were all snuggled up to him, and ready for the story.

"I was there," he began, and those magic words sent shivers down my spine. It was going to be the wizard story. "Dorothy and me were both there. She never tells Uncle Henry or Aunt Em this story any more, because they won't believe her. She told me that one day, when she has children of her own, she'll tell them, because children know how to believe. Well, pups are children too, right? So I can tell you. Think of that: you little pups will know this story before any people folks know it, except Dorothy, of course, and me."

We were all silent, snuggled up together, all of us lying there, waiting, waiting. Then Papa Toto began.

"Well, little pups, my tale begins in this very house, in this very room, in this very basket...

CHAPTER ONE

———◆———

A Giant Monster
of a Twister

I was lying right here, deep in my dreams in this very basket, when I was woken up by the sound of the wind roaring and howling around the house, rattling the doors and windows, shaking the whole place. I never heard a wind like it. The door blew open. So I got up and went outside. Everyone was rushing round, Dorothy trying to shut the hens into the hen house, but they were skittering about all over the place.

They didn't want to go inside, of course they didn't. It wasn't getting dark yet. The hens never go to bed before dark. What was Dorothy thinking of? Uncle Henry was driving the cattle into the barn, but they didn't want to go in either, and he was calling for me to come and help him, but I had sleep still in my head and didn't want to. Anyway, he was managing well enough on his own, I thought, without me. Aunt Em was trying to shut the barn doors, but the wind wouldn't let her. She was blown off her feet and went rolling over and over, like tumbleweed. Dorothy saw what was happening, left her hens and ran to help Aunt Em up on to her feet, and together with Uncle Henry they managed to shut the barn door.

Then they did some more chasing round, getting old Barney, our plough horse, into his stable, rounding up the pigs – and that wasn't easy either – and all the while they were hollering at each other about a great storm coming in, and how the clouds were dark in the north and how that was a bad sign.

"If I'm not mistaken, there's a twister on the way," Uncle Henry was bellowing. "I'll eat my hat else."

And then suddenly he didn't
have any hat on his head any more.
It had blown away. So I went after it.

I love a good old hat chase, especially when there's a wind blowing over the prairies in Kansas. As Uncle Henry often says, maybe other folks in other places invented the wheel and writing and all that clever stuff, but in Kansas we invented the wind.

Anyways, I went chasing that hat of Uncle Henry's just about all over Kansas, and caught up with it down by the creek where it landed in the water, and I dived right in, grabbed it in my teeth and trotted back home, head high, tail high, pretty darned pleased with myself.

I've always been like that. If I'm chasing after something, hats especially, I put just about everyone and everything else out of my mind. But now the chase was over and I could hear Dorothy screaming for me to come home. I could see her now, standing on the veranda of the farmhouse, and right behind her and nearly right above her came this giant monster of a twister just a-roaring and a-raging, towering up into the sky, taking the barn with it, making splinters of it, and the fences too, and the rain tub, swirling and swallowing the lot. Well, I ran. I took the steps up the veranda in one bound, jumped right into Dorothy's arms.

"Where've you been, Toto?" she cried, hugging me to her and running into the house.

I showed her the hat in my mouth, shook it for her to be quite sure she noticed how clever I had been!

"You rescued Uncle Henry's hat!" I was so pleased that she was pleased. "You are such a clever Toto. Don't you drop it now. We got to get ourselves safe out of this storm, else we'll be blowed to smithereens. Aunt Em and Uncle Henry are waiting for us down in the cellar. But I couldn't really leave you behind, could I? I ain't going down there without Toto, I told them. And now I got you, that's where we're going, right now. I know you don't like it down in the dark, Toto, but it's safe down there, so like it or lump it, you're coming with me."

She was right, I hated it down in that cellar. Never did like the dark, still don't. I could see the trapdoor open on the far side of the room. I could hear Aunt Em and Uncle Henry hollering for us to hurry up. Dorothy managed to get the front door shut against the wind, with the house shaking all around us, shaking so bad I thought that old twister was going to make splinters of it any moment. Cups and saucers, jugs and plates, smashed on to the floor. Drawers flew open, knives and forks and spoons, kettles and pots and pans, rattled and crashed, chairs and cupboards and dressers tipped over.

I was never so scared in all my life. We were halfway across the room when the strangest thing happened. The trapdoor slammed itself shut, and all of a sudden the shaking and the roaring, the whistling and wailing, simply stopped. I heard Aunt Em and Uncle Henry still calling for us from down below in the cellar, but their voices were becoming fainter with every moment.

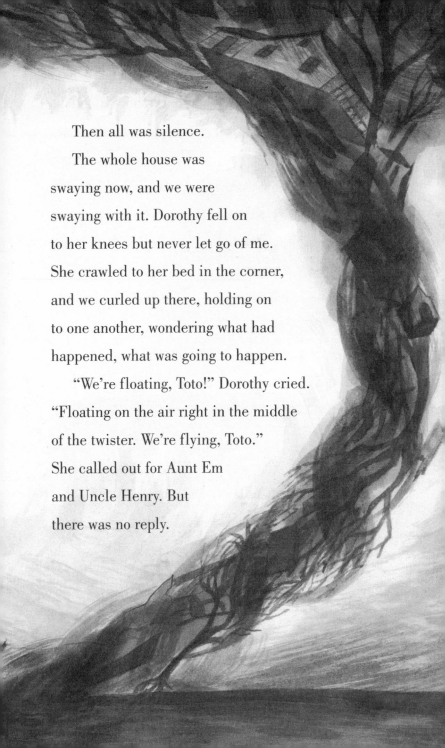

Then all was silence.

The whole house was
swaying now, and we were
swaying with it. Dorothy fell on
to her knees but never let go of me.
She crawled to her bed in the corner,
and we curled up there, holding on
to one another, wondering what had
happened, what was going to happen.

"We're floating, Toto!" Dorothy cried.
"Floating on the air right in the middle
of the twister. We're flying, Toto."
She called out for Aunt Em
and Uncle Henry. But
there was no reply.

"We're all alone," Dorothy said, her voice trembling a bit. "But don't you worry none. I'll look after you, Toto. You know I will."

And I did know that, so I wasn't worried, not as much as I had been anyway. There was blue sky outside the window now, and we were flying up and out of the clouds. There was hardly a sound. I wasn't frightened at all any more. I did feel a little sick though, what with all this floating about in the air, especially when the house lurched and tipped and rocked about.

"We'd best lie down, Toto," said Dorothy, "and close our eyes, then we'll feel better."

So that's what we did, and pretty soon, what with all that gentle swaying and rocking, we were both of us fast asleep, her arm around me, my head in her lap, Uncle Henry's hat right beside me. She'd told me to look after his hat, so that's just what I was doing.

CHAPTER TWO

Landing in the Land of the Munchkins

I always slept on Dorothy's bed – Aunt Em and Uncle Henry didn't like me to, but I often snuck up on to her bed when they were asleep. Then Dorothy was happy, and I was happy. We breathed together. I think sometimes we dreamed the same dream together. I was usually awake before her. She was a bit of a sleepyhead. But this time we were woken up together by the same jarring, crashing bump. We sat up at once.

The house didn't like it any more than we did. The whole place groaned and creaked around us. And then we heard nothing for a while except the sound of whispering outside the farmhouse door. Strangers!

I don't like strangers, especially not whispering strangers. I leapt off the bed, barking as fiercely as I could, just to let them know how terrifying I can be, which is never easy for me because, as you know, little puppies, I am a small black dog with a yappy kind of a bark. Very likely you'll be much the same when you grow up. I can point my tail, make the hair stand up along my back like a bottle brush, and I can bare my teeth. I can frighten rats and rabbits and cats and the like. But, if I'm honest, the most frightening thing about me is probably my cold, cold nose. Wake up Dorothy or Aunt Em or Uncle Henry with my cold, cold nose, and they shriek like blue murder. Of course, my nose was no use to me with these whispering strangers on the other side of the door. But luckily they couldn't see how small I was. I barked and growled as deep as

I could, howled like a bloodhound, snarled like a wolf.

Dorothy was beside me, and she could hear the whispering too. "Who's out there?" she cried.

"Only us," came a friendly voice at last. "We are the Munchkins!"

Dorothy opened the door and I went bounding out, barking my head off. I was so amazed by what I saw that I stopped barking at once. Standing on the grass just beyond the veranda steps was the strangest crowd of people, every one of them with a round-brimmed hat, dressed in azure blue, and all the size of children – Dorothy's size – but with grown-up faces. All of them looked like men people folk, except one, a little old lady, and she had long white hair. Her face was as wrinkled and brown as an autumn leaf. She was the one who spoke first. She was pointing at me, which was rather rude, I thought.

"What is that?" she asked, wrinkling her nose. "And who are you?"

"I am Dorothy," Dorothy told her. "And this is Toto, my dog, and my best friend, and he does not bite."

"I never saw such a dog before. An odd-looking creature," the strange lady went on. "But if he is your best friend he is most welcome, as you are. We all of us want to thank you from the bottom of our hearts."

"What for?" Dorothy asked.

"For coming here and saving us, of course! For killing the Wicked Witch of the East, my dear."

"Killing her! But I've never killed anything in all my life," Dorothy protested. "Toto here will go after a rabbit or a mouse, maybe, or a hat. But that is his nature; what dogs do. I've never killed anything. I wouldn't hurt a fly or a beetle or any living creature."

"Well, maybe you haven't, but your house has," replied the old lady. "Look, over there!" She was pointing at the corner of the house. "See those two feet sticking out from under the house? That is all that is left of her, the Wicked Witch of the East. Her two pointed feet and her two red shoes. She's done for.

30

You squashed her good and proper, or rather your house did."

"Oh my goodness!" cried Dorothy. The tears were coming, and she could not stop them. "I'm so very sorry. I can't believe it. I never meant to do such a terrible thing."

But the strange old lady shook her head. "Don't be upset, my dear, you have done a good thing, though you didn't know it. It's the Wicked Witch of the East, who was cruel and terrible. She was the wickedest witch that ever lived. Think of it this way: your house has saved many lives."

Dorothy looked uncertain.

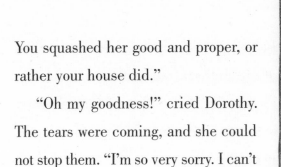

"You must believe me, my dear. Your house did us all a great favour," said the old lady. "Didn't it, Munchkins?" All the Munchkins whispered their appreciation, nodding very vigorously and clapping most enthusiastically.

"You can see they are happy, as I am too," she went on, "because these poor unfortunate Munchkins have slaved for that horrible Wicked Witch of the East, day and night, all their lives. They were under her wicked spell, which is now all over, because she is dead, dead as a doornail."

"So she really was a witch? She could put spells on people?" Dorothy asked.

"Yes," replied the old lady. "But witches are not all wicked like she was. I am a witch myself, but I am not a wicked one, am I, Munchkins?" And all the Munchkins whispered amongst themselves – their whispering sounded like a wind blowing through the trees – and then shook their heads all together. "I can make spells, as all witches can," she went on.

"But I make only good spells."

"You are a real live witch?" gasped Dorothy, stepping back a pace, and wiping the tears from her cheeks.

"Oh yes, my dear, I am the Good Witch of the North. But there is nothing to be frightened of," she said. "You should have known my dear sister, the Good Witch of the South. She was killed by another Wicked Witch, the wickedest witch who ever lived, and the sister of this one you squashed with your house. Another reason I have – we all have – to thank you. She and I, we did all we could to help and protect good and kind people like the Munchkins, to save them from the Wicked Witches of the East and the West. We wanted to set them free, but our power was not strong enough. And then out of the blue your house comes falling down out of the sky and squashes the Wicked Witch of the East, and now the Munchkins are free, thanks to you."

"I don't understand," Dorothy said. "My Aunt Em back in Kansas, where I live, she says that all witches

are make-believe, that they are only in story books, and not real at all."

"Well, your little dog thinks I'm real, don't you?" the old lady said. And it was true. I was sniffing her hand and she smelt real enough to me, quite sweet, like syrup. I like syrup. "Nice dog. Cold nose. I like a dog with a cold nose that wags her tail. Where is this Kansas place you came from? I have not heard of it."

"Toto is a he not a she," said Dorothy. "And Kansas is – I don't know – up there somewhere in the sky, I suppose. It's where we live, Toto and me, and we want to go home. I mean, you folk look really nice, and I can tell now, like Toto can, that you are a good witch. But we don't have real witches, good or wicked, unless they are in books, and Aunt Em says they can't do much harm in books.

"I mean, you just close the book, and poof! The wicked witch or the magic-making wizard, or whatever, is gone. Aunt Em and Uncle Henry will be mighty worried on account of the farmhouse flying off with us in it. Can't you please help us get back home?"

"Well, I can't do it," said the Good Witch of the North. "But there is someone I know who might..."

"Oh, please, do tell us!" said Dorothy. "I so wish to go home."

"There is a wizard we know," the Good Witch of the North went on thoughtfully. "Isn't there, Munchkins?" The Munchkins all trembled terribly at this and whispered frantically. "He is called the Wizard of Oz. He is a great and terrible and powerful wizard, and he lives far away in the Emerald City, down the yellow brick road, which is a very long road. No one is wiser, I have heard. No one is cleverer. He knows everything there is to know. He'll know for sure how to get you back to your home in this Kansas place – though why you ever should wish to leave this beautiful country of ours, I can't imagine, especially now that you have killed the Wicked Witch of the East. Look around you. This will be such a happy country now after what you have done, as happy as it is beautiful. And, believe me, the Munchkins are the kindest folk who ever lived."

Until then I don't think either Dorothy or I had even noticed just how beautiful this place where we had landed was. Everywhere we looked there were grassy meadows full of wild and wonderful flowers, and forests of towering trees, luscious fruits growing from them, and leaves all the colours of the rainbow. There were bubbling, sparkling streams, humming bees and fluttering butterflies. And every bird that flew overhead was like a bright jewel, and sang so sweetly. Gone was the flat, grey land of the prairies of Kansas, the dusty tracks, the cruel wind and the tumbleweed.

"It is so beautiful," said Dorothy, "but home

is home, and home is best."

"You're so dog-gone right," I woofed.

Just then the Munchkins began to whisper and point excitedly at the corner of the house. "All gone, all gone," they muttered in unison.

Those pointed feet sticking out from under the house had gone, disappeared, vanished entirely. Only the Wicked Witch's red shoes were left. I went to sniff around – my nose tells me so much more than my eyes ever do. Dust, all I could smell was dust. I picked up a shoe and carried it back to Dorothy, who sat down right away and

put it on: "Just the right size," she  said, "and so comfortable it's as if they were made for me."

"They are yours now, my dear," said the kindly Witch of the North. "The nasty Witch of the East always wore those shoes because there is magic power in them.

"But magic obeys only the heart of the one who uses it. Your magic would always be a kind magic, because you are kind, I can tell. Please stay and help us."

"I would..." said Dorothy, and I could hear the wobble in her voice, so I knew she was going to cry. I know Dorothy so well. I always knew – I still do – when she is happy before she is happy, when she is sad before she is sad. "And I do love my new shoes, truly I do... but I do so want to go home. Aunt Em and Uncle Henry are the only family I've got. Please tell me how to get back home. If you are a good witch, you must know the way."

But all the Munchkins were shaking their heads and crying because she was crying. I touched her leg with my cold, cold nose and wagged my tail and looked up into her eyes to comfort her.

"There is only one thing for it, Dorothy, my dear," the old lady said, stroking Dorothy's hair and wiping her eyes with her handkerchief. "You must go to the Wizard of Oz, who knows everything. You must follow the yellow brick road."

"Follow the yellow brick road?" echoed Dorothy.

"Yes," said the kindly Witch of the North. "To see the Wizard of Oz."

"You called him terrible. Is he a good man or a wicked man?" Dorothy asked.

"He is terribly powerful, but everyone says he is a good wizard. However, I have to say I have never met him. I don't even know what he looks like. No one does. But, if you want to go home to this *Kansas*, he's the only one who can help you. It is a long way to go, but an easy road to follow. Just follow the yellow brick road and you will find the Emerald City. But look after yourself – there will be great dangers on the way. Remember, the right road is never the easy road. But you will look after her, Toto, won't you? Can you be ferocious and fierce?"

I growled my best to show her, straightened my tail, and rose up the hackles along my back like a bottle brush. I bared my teeth. The Munchkins shrank back in horror and fear, and I was, I am ashamed to say, rather pleased with myself about that. *I may be small and funny-looking, I thought, but I can still make like a wicked wolf when I need to.*

Dorothy tickled the top of my head with her fingers, which is always her way of telling me to calm down and be nice. The Good Witch of the North bent forward and kissed Dorothy softly on her forehead.

"The mark of my lips will stay there for as long as you need protection. Now you have a kiss from

the Good Witch of the North, no one who sees it will dare harm you. And you have good magic in your red shoes. Be brave, Dorothy, my dear. Look after her, Toto. Goodbye now. You follow the stream through the trees and you'll soon come to the yellow brick road."

She turned about three times on her left heel and simply vanished into thin air. The Munchkins bowed silently, and went off over the grass meadow, whispering amongst themselves and looking back at us as they went, before they too disappeared into the long grass and the flowers. I thought at first it was the flowers themselves that were singing. But it was Munchkins, I'm sure of it.

"Follow the yellow brick road," they sang. "Follow the yellow brick road."

"Well then, Toto," said Dorothy, "up we get and off we go! Home is home, and home is best."

"You're so dog-gone right," I woofed.

CHAPTER THREE

A Real Live Walking,
Talking Scarecrow

*B*y now, my little puppies, I was getting pretty hungry, I can tell you...

I was especially missing the sausages that Aunt Em always made for breakfast. Uncle Henry would often sneak me one under the table; Dorothy too. But Aunt Em never. I do love my sausages.

I tried all sorts to let Dorothy know. I sat down right by her all polite and tail tucked in, and touched her with my cold, cold nose. That didn't

work. I looked up at her as plaintively as I could – and I can do plaintive pretty darned well when I want to, little puppies – and all the while letting my tongue hang out and dribble. I did a bit of whining and whimpering. I tried pawing her leg. But she was just too busy to pay me much attention.

"Not now, Toto," Dorothy said. "Can't you see I'm getting myself dressed and all smartened up for our long walk down the yellow brick road?" She was putting on her favourite frock, of blue and white checks. "Doesn't it look fine, Toto, with my new red shoes?" she said, twirling round to show me. "And look," she said, tying her bonnet on, "better still with my bonnet that Aunt Em made especially! And my basket too for sandwiches. We've got to have sandwiches. And we'll put Uncle Henry's hat in the basket too, so we won't forget it."

I sat there, telling her with my eyes as best I could that I really wasn't that interested in her bonnet or her basket, that my tummy was gurgling and groaning with hunger. Finally, finally, she got the message.

"Oh, Toto! I'm sorry. Don't look so sad. Aunt Em had some ham and bread in the kitchen. I'll soon find something for you." Now she was talking! She made ham sandwiches on the kitchen table. There were broken plates and dishes scattered all around us; everything was topsy-turvy. That twister had surely made a dreadful mess of the place. Dorothy had a sandwich and I had one too. I had lots! She made a few more for the journey. I thanked her with my eyes, with my dribbly tongue, and with my cold, cold nose. "Now we have to find the yellow brick road," Dorothy said, "which will lead us, so that kind Good Witch said, to the Emerald City and the Great and Terrible Wizard of Oz. I don't much like the sound of 'terrible', Toto. But just so long as he can help us get back to Kansas, we don't care how terrible he is, do we, Toto?"

So she picked up her basket, now with Uncle Henry's hat in it, and packed it with some more sandwiches. Sadly there were no sausages.

Off we went then, shutting the door behind us, following the stream, where I stopped to have a long, cool drink. Dorothy said I made a lot of noise with my lapping, as if I wanted to drink the whole stream. Well, the water was lovely, and I love to lap.

We walked on and on through lovely leafy orchards of apples and pears and peaches and plums, where Dorothy helped herself and filled her basket, being careful not to squash Uncle Henry's hat.

To be honest, I'm not that keen on fruit, never have been. And, at last, there ahead of us lay the yellow brick road, golden in sunshine, stretching away over the hills into the distance as far as the eye could see.

"Come along, Toto," Dorothy said. "That's the way we go, that's our way home to Kansas, back home to Aunt Em and Uncle Henry."

So there we were, the two of us, Dorothy carrying the basket over her arm with the ham sandwiches in it, and the fruit she picked on the way, making our way along the yellow brick road. She was happy, I could tell, skipping along, and singing as she went. So I was happy too, because she was, and because we were on our way home, with a little bit of luck.

All the Munchkins we met along the way could not have been kinder. They all seemed to know what we had done, or the farmhouse had done, how we had squashed the Wicked Witch of the East and set them free. They gave us shelter for the night. They feted us, feasted us royally. There was dancing and singing wherever we went. I loved playing with the children, and they made a great fuss of me, squeaking with laughter when I jumped for their balls or leapt into the stream after their sticks. The Munchkins would hang garlands around our necks, before setting us on our way again the next day, waving us off, wishing us well. Those Munchkin folk thought I was the funniest thing they had ever seen – I don't think any of them had ever seen a dog before. The babies and toddlers in particular loved me, pulling my tail and ears, never too hard. And I'd let them, because it didn't hurt, and they'd giggle and gurgle and shriek.

And they all loved Dorothy too, because they knew she was a kind and good witch – she had to be, they said, because she had killed the Wicked Witch of the East, which was good, and set them free, which was good. And they also said there were blue checks in her dress, and blue was the Munchkins' favourite colour. They too all wore blue dresses or blue jackets and trousers, blue hats, and blue socks and shoes. So for many reasons they felt Dorothy was one of them. They loved her when she danced, loved her when she sang. I have to say, I have always thought Dorothy sings a bit shrilly and squeakily for my liking, and she sings a little too often as well, but they seemed to like it.

But once we were on our way again, down the yellow brick road, Dorothy fell silent. Dorothy wasn't often silent. Something was wrong.

She soon told me what it was. "No one seems to know how far it is to the Emerald City, and all the Munchkins say we should be very careful, that everything may look mighty pretty on the way, but there will be dangers ahead, that we have to be brave, and I'm not sure I'm all that brave, Toto. And they all seem terribly frightened of the Wizard of Oz, whenever they speak of him. I don't know why. But we have to find him, Toto, don't we? He's the only one who can help us get back to Kansas. And I want to see Aunt Em again and Uncle Henry. So we'll just have to be brave, won't we, Toto? We'll walk on down the yellow brick road for as long as it takes and we won't be frightened, not of anyone, not of anything, and especially not of the Wizard of Oz." That's how Dorothy always cheered herself up, by talking to herself, or to me – to both of us mostly.

So on we went, under the hot, hot sun, Dorothy skipping along, singing rather too often, and me trotting along cheerily at her heels, wagging my tail to keep happy and keep her happy too. After a few miles we sat down by a stream to rest. She was dabbling her aching feet in the cool of the stream, and I was lapping up all the water I could.

"Look!" cried Dorothy suddenly. "Over there! A scarecrow! Like we have at home on the farm." And, sure enough, a little further down the stream, standing in a field of ripe corn, was a scarecrow, but he was not at all like the poor old stuffed sack of a scarecrow we had back home, with Uncle Henry's dirty old hat and dusty old jacket, and his smelly old pipe stuck in his mouth.

No, this was the smartest-looking scarecrow I ever saw. He had proper eyes and a proper nose and a proper mouth. He even had sticks for ears. He was dressed like the Munchkins, entirely in blue, wore the same kind of round, wide-brimmed hat they did, that was pointed at the top, and was blue like everything else he wore. He had proper boots on him too, like the Munchkins, blue ones, and blue socks too.

"Why, he looks almost alive!" cried Dorothy. "What a fine scarecrow!" We got up and ran down along the riverbank to get a closer look. Dorothy was right. He was the finest scarecrow I ever saw. He wasn't at all lopsided and weather-beaten like the poor old fellow back home. This one stood up straight and tall.

As we came closer, we could see he had a pole stuck under his jacket at the back, fixing him securely to the ground. He was standing there stiff and still, but he was so real-looking, so alive-looking. I ran up to him, barking at him. He never moved, so I knew he had to be a scarecrow, a smart scarecrow, but a scarecrow like all scarecrows: a stuffed-with-straw man.

"Hello, little dog," he said suddenly.

The scarecrow spoke!

He was alive!

D orothy looked at me. I looked at Dorothy.

"'Scuse me, sir," Dorothy said, "but did you speak?"

"I did," came the reply. His voice sounded much as how you would expect a scarecrow to speak, with a rather husky, dusty voice. Dorothy didn't seem to know what to say. I did. I just went on barking till she shushed me. Then she said what all people folk seem to say when they don't know what else to say. "How are you doing, sir?"

"Not so good, I'm afraid," said the scarecrow. "I mean, all I do is stand here all day and all night. I don't just scare away crows – that's my job – I scare away everything and everyone. It gets a bit lonely, if I'm honest. I'm not complaining, mind. My Munchkin farmer comes out to see me from time to time and tells me his troubles, says he likes talking to me because I'm a good friend and I listen. Back home, he says, no one listens to him."

"Poor you," Dorothy said. "Can't you move? Just

walk away?"

"I wish, how I wish. See this pole stuck up my jacket? Well, it's hammered deep into the ground behind me. So I'm stuck here, can't move."

"Have you asked the farmer to let you go?" said Dorothy. "Uncle Henry's a farmer and he's very kind. Most farmers are, in Kansas."

"Oh, I've asked him," said the scarecrow. "But he says he made me so I belong here, that I have a job to do, and besides he likes my company."

"That doesn't seem very fair," said Dorothy. "Wouldn't you like to be free?"

"More than anything," said the scarecrow. "But how can I get myself off this pole? I can't move."

"We'll soon fix that," Dorothy told him, "won't we, Toto?"

"Toto?" the scarecrow asked.

"That's my dog's name, and I'm Dorothy," Dorothy said, tugging at the pole, and wiggling it back and forth, to and fro. "Have you got a name?"

"Just Scarecrow," said Scarecrow. "It's what I am, just an old scarecrow stuffed with straw. You'll never get that pole out of the ground, Dorothy. It's very kind of you to try. Maybe you could lift me off? I'm very light, you'll see." So Dorothy reached up, put her arms right around him and lifted him clear of the pole, then set him down on the ground in front of her. I expected him to fall over, but he didn't. He shook himself down, pulled his coat straight and arranged his hat. "There," he said, "that's much better. I feel quite a new scarecrow. You've been so good to me, Dorothy. Thank you so very much." He looked down at me, as if he was rather nervous of me. "Does that dog bite?" he asked.

"Never," Dorothy replied, which was not quite true. "And anyway, Toto likes you. I like you."

"And I like you too, both of you," Scarecrow said. "So where were you off to this fine day, if I might ask?"

Dorothy told him where we had come from and where we were going and why, and all about the Great and Terrible Wizard of Oz who could do just about everything, make anything happen, because his magic was so powerful. Scarecrow didn't seem in the least bit frightened by the mention of the Wizard of Oz, as so many of the Munchkins had been.

"I wonder," he said, "might I come along with you perhaps? I've been standing here in this field for a week or two now, and I've never done any walking. I'd love to go for a long walk, wherever it takes me. It would be good for me, loosen me up.

And I should love to have new friends."

I was sniffing at Scarecrow now. He smelt just like the barn back home in Kansas, a good familiar smell, a strong whiff of Uncle Henry's trousers, and pipe tobacco, and rather of mice too. I like mice and rats, to chase I mean. Dorothy was right, I did like Scarecrow, and I liked his smells! "Of course you can come with us, can't he, Toto?" said Dorothy. "I think that would be a fine idea. Let's go, shall we?"

So the three of us set off down the yellow brick road that wound its way into the far, far distance, the two of them chatting away beside me as we went. "Maybe you can help, Scarecrow," Dorothy said after a while. "You see, Toto and I, we do not know this country at all. This yellow brick road looks as if it will go on for ever. Do you happen to know how far it is to the Emerald City?"

Until now Scarecrow had been walking along quite happily, but suddenly he stopped and stood there,

shaking his head sadly. "I wish I could help you, Dorothy," he said, "but look at me. I know nothing. I am made of straw, all of me, my legs, my arms, my body, and worst of all, my head. I have no brains in my head at all, only straw. Maybe the Great and Terrible Wizard of Oz, if he can do just about everything he wants to do like you say, could give me some brains? I want brains in my head like you, so I can know things, understand things. Everyone thinks I'm stupid, and I am, I am."

"No, Scarecrow, you're not," Dorothy said, holding his hands and looking up into his eyes. "You are good and kind and gentle, and Aunt Em says that's more important than anything else, doesn't she, Toto?"

I jumped up on Scarecrow's leg and licked his hand, to make him feel happier. And that's when I smelt a stronger whiff of mice and rats in his straw, and so I snuffled at him with my nose, growling just a little, because I was so excited. I get like that when I smell a rat or a mouse.

"He's growling at me," said Scarecrow.

"Don't be afraid," Dorothy told him. "Toto won't hurt you."

"Oh, I'm not afraid of dogs, Dorothy," Scarecrow said. "I'm not afraid of anything – oh, except fire. I really don't like fire. I can't think why, but I don't like fire at all. Maybe fire and straw don't agree with one another somehow. I don't know. That's my trouble, Dorothy, that's what's wrong with me, you see? No brains. I don't know anything."

CHAPTER FOUR

How the Three of us Became Four

So now, little puppies – and I do wish some of you would stop wriggling so; it puts me off, makes me forget where I am in the story – so now there were the three of us, all together, following the yellow brick road towards the Emerald City to see the Great and Terrible Wizard of Oz. And our new-found friend Scarecrow turned out to be the best of companions, in one way especially. He did not eat – scarecrows don't need to, apparently –

which meant that Dorothy and I could share those few sandwiches that were in her basket, so there was more for each of us, more for me!

And, like Dorothy, Scarecrow loved to natter away, to tell stories. There was never a dull moment. I sniffed and snuffled along the roadside as we went, loving all the new smells of this strange place, missing some of the old whiffs of course – no whiff of rabbit here, no whiff of squirrel, or hedgehog, no whiff of sausages, either. But I didn't mind, I had Dorothy and Scarecrow to listen to as we walked along.

Walking, it soon turned out, wasn't at all easy for Scarecrow. He kept staggering about and tripping over and falling. "I am not used to this walking lark," he explained as Dorothy helped him up yet again on to his feet. "I am used to standing still. But don't worry. It doesn't hurt when I fall over, not one bit."

Dorothy took his arm anyway to steady him, to help him on, but mostly I could see it was because she liked him. She talked to him more about how we had got

here and all about home and Kansas and
Aunt Em and Uncle Henry, and about how
much she missed them and how much she
wanted to go home. "Home is home," she said,
"and home is best."

"You're so dog-gone right," I woofed.

"And besides," said Dorothy, "Uncle Henry must
be missing his hat by now. We have to get it back
to him."

"Hat?" said Scarecrow.

Dorothy took Uncle Henry's hat out of the basket
and held it up.

"It's a long story," said Dorothy, and she gave it to
me to carry for a while. Made me feel right at home,
trotting along with Uncle Henry's hat in my mouth.
"We've just got to get home, that's all."

"Well, if you'll forgive me for saying so, Dorothy,"
Scarecrow said, "I can't imagine why you would ever
want to leave this beautiful country, to go back to that
grey old Kansas and those horrible twisters and the

like. From the way you tell it, it sounds a most dreadful place. I mean, just look around you. Isn't this the most lovely of places, with the kindest of people? And you want to leave it and go back to that wind and all that tumbleweed? I don't understand you at all, I really don't. But then I don't understand anything, do I? I wouldn't, would I, because I have no brains. My head is stuffed with straw like the rest of me. Well, I think it's lucky for Kansas that you want to live there, because you are a good and kind person. And countries need good and kind folk. Lucky Kansas! Lucky Kansas!"

And Scarecrow skipped along with Dorothy for a while, both of them, chanting "Lucky Kansas, Lucky Kansas" over and over, till Scarecrow tripped and stumbled and nearly fell over himself again. They were a bit breathless after that and so they sat down to rest by a stream.

I wasn't breathless at all, so I went exploring. There was a smell about the place I recognised, the same smell as Uncle Henry's saw in the barn back home, the same smell as his scythe and his great heavy fencing hammer. It was definitely the smell of metal. But strong though the smell was, I couldn't see anything that was made of metal anywhere. I followed the scent of it, but lost it. So in the end I got fed up looking and went to sit down with them by the stream, where I found Scarecrow telling Dorothy his story.

"Truth to tell, I was only made a week or two ago," he was saying. "The Munchkin farmer who made me, painted me ears and eyes to hear and see with, a nose to smell with, and a mouth to talk with. He took great care. He said he thought I would like to see how the rest of me was made as he was making me. He's a very thoughtful and good man, as I think I've told you. And it was interesting, if a little strange, to watch the rest of me coming together, taking shape, my arms and legs and body being stitched up and stuffed, then all my clothes put on me. The bit I didn't like so much was when he stuck a pole up the back of my jacket, and carried me out into the field, then hammered me in

and left me, telling me to be a good
scarecrow and frighten off all the crows so
they didn't fly down and eat his corn.

"I was pretty good at it too at first, frightened them
all silly I did. But then this old crow came flying along
and landed on top of my head. 'You don't fool me,' he
cawed. 'You're not a proper Munchkin at all. You're
nothing but an old sack stuffed with straw, aren't you,
not a brain in your head. Couldn't hurt a fly, could you?
Doesn't matter whether you be a bird like me or a man
like a Munchkin, you've got no brains. Now if you had
brains, you could be of some use. As it is, you're just
a brainless, worthless scarecrow, no use to anyone.'
And, of course, that old crow was right. Soon he was
helping himself to the corn all around my feet, and there
was nothing I could do about it. Then all the birds for
miles around arrived and were pecking away happily. I
couldn't even do my job, not without a brain, could I?
The poor old Munchkin farmer was nice enough about
it. 'Not your fault,' he told me. 'Maybe I didn't make you

right. Not your fault you haven't got any brains, is it?'"

Dorothy tried to cheer him up, as best she could. "As soon as we get to the Emerald City, as soon as we see the Great and Terrible Wizard of Oz, we'll put that right," she said. "You'll see. You'll have your brains. Don't let's be downhearted. Up we get and off we go."

So on we went.

Now, people folk – and scarecrows come to that – don't seem to see so well in the dark as we dogs do. So it was me that found the cottage in the wood, or rather my nose did, I should say. I've got a good nose, just about the best nose there is, if I say it myself. That metal scent I'd discovered a while before, well, I picked it up again, and it led me right to the door of this cottage, which was rather strange as it was built entirely of wood, and when we went inside I saw that all the furniture was made of wood as well. I was really puzzled by that. But Dorothy and Scarecrow were delighted with the place. We were so tired with all that walking. All we wanted to do was sleep. It was dry and clean, and there was a soft bed of dried leaves in the corner for Dorothy and me. I curled up beside her. Scarecrow stayed standing by the window. He said he preferred to stand; he was used to it, and didn't sleep anyway.

"I don't understand what sleep is for," he said.

"You will," murmured Dorothy beside me, already half asleep, "just as soon as you have some brains. And you soon will have. Goodnight, Scarecrow."

"Goodnight, Dorothy," he replied. "Goodnight, Toto."

I woke up early. Scarecrow opened the door for me and out I went to explore the woods. That metal smell was stronger still.

I had to find out what it was, but the scent took me round in circles and brought me right back to the cottage. Dorothy was up, searching the cottage for something to eat. The sandwiches and the fruit were all finished by now. Her basket was empty apart from Uncle Henry's hat, and the cupboards were all bare.

All she could find was an oil can on a shelf.

"We can't eat oil, can we? We shall have to find food somewhere soon, I'm so hungry," she said, going outside. "Or we'll starve. Come on, we're bound to find some fruit or some nuts. There are trees everywhere here." So we walked off into the woods looking for fruit or nuts, anything we could find. But there was nothing. "These are just forest trees," Dorothy said. "Not fruit trees or nut trees. What are we going to do?"

I thought, when I first heard it, that it was Dorothy groaning with hunger, but it wasn't. She was looking at me, and so was Scarecrow.

"Did you groan, Toto?" she said. The groaning was louder now, and closer. It wasn't her doing it, not Scarecrow, not me. And then through the trees, I saw something ahead of us in a clearing, a-glinting it was, and a-shining. It was something metal! I know metal when I smell it. My trusty nose! It never lets me down! I was off, following my nose.

Dorothy and Scarecrow were coming along some way behind, so I got there first.

In the clearing stood a man made entirely of tin, an axe raised above his head and about to chop down a tree. It was half chopped down already. He stood as still as a statue. But then the tin woodman groaned. I ran up to him. He smelt like Uncle Henry's saw, like his scythe, like his hammer, yes, and like his axe too. I bit the man's leg then, just to let him know that he wasn't to harm Dorothy. It hurt my teeth, so I didn't do it again. I barked instead, loudly, sharply, pointed my tail, bared my teeth, made my hackles rise like a bottle brush all along my back, just so he got the message.

"Oh, hello, little dog," said the man of tin, and I backed away, frightened. Though I suppose I should have been used to strange talking creatures by then.

Dorothy was so brave though. She walked right up to him: "Was it you groaning?"

"I've been standing here like this, groaning for a year or more," he replied, "and no one has ever heard

me before. I am so glad you came." His voice echoed and boomed inside him as he spoke.

"Are you stuck or something?" Dorothy asked. "Why is everyone around here so stuck? Can we help you?"

"That is kind of you," he replied. "I need to be oiled. My can of oil, it's in my cabin. I should be so obliged if you would fetch it for me."

"I saw it, I know where it is," said Dorothy. "I'll fetch it. Don't go away." And off she ran back through the wood."I may be brainless," said Scarecrow, "but I don't think you could go away, Mr Tin Man, even if you wanted to, could you?"

"Quite right," said the tin man.

While we waited for Dorothy, Scarecrow and the tin man chatted away as if they had been friends for a long time, comparing notes as to whether it was better to be made of tin or straw.

"Well, at least you can't rust up like me," said the tin man. "I don't like rain."

"Well, at least you can't catch fire like me," said Scarecrow. "I don't like fire."

Dorothy was soon back, and she set to at once, oiling the tin man's neck so he could begin to move his head, turn it this way and that, shake it, nod it. Scarecrow took hold of his head and helped to loosen it gently. Then Dorothy oiled his arms and his legs, and his hips as well. Soon he could move his knees and his elbows quite freely, and could lower the axe, wiggle and wriggle and jiggle just about everything he needed to. He danced up and down in sheer delight. "You have saved my life, my dear friends," he said. "But what are you doing here in the forest? How did you find me? My name is Tin Woodman. I live in that cottage. But who are you?" So they all shook hands there in the forest, and introduced themselves. I have to say, I felt rather left out at that moment. So I reminded Dorothy I was there, loudly.

"Toto was the one who found you, Tin Woodman," said Dorothy. "I'm sorry he bit you, but he gets rather excited sometimes, I'm afraid." And then she told him the whole story of how we were there in the Land of Oz, and how we were on our way to see the Great and Terrible Wizard, who knows everything, and can do everything, and who could help us get home to Kansas. "Home is home," said Dorothy, "and home is best."

"You're so dog-gone right," I woofed.

"What I need is not a home but a heart," sighed Tin Woodman. "If only I could come with you, I could ask him, couldn't I? He could give me a heart. He's a kindly sort of wizard, isn't he?"

"I hope so," said Scarecrow, "or I'll never have any brains."

"Of course you can come along," said Dorothy. "The more the merrier — as Aunt Em always says when she's collecting the eggs. As for the Great Wizard of Oz, let us hope he is kind, but I have heard he is also terrible."

"Oh, I don't care. This is the very best day of my life!" cried Tin Woodman happily, and off he clanked through the trees, dancing a little jig as he went. "I can walk, look at me! I can dance, look at me! And I have new friends,

and I'm going to have a heart. With a bit of luck." He stopped and turned round. "Don't forget the oil can, Dorothy. If I get caught in the rain, I'll rust up and go all stiff again, and I don't want that."

So Dorothy put the oil can in her basket, and off we went after Tin Woodman till we came out of the wood at last and found the yellow brick road again, me trotting along in front, tail waving, nose to the ground, sniffing out whatever smelt interesting. And in this place every smell was more than interesting. But nothing here smelt quite like Kansas. Even the rats and mice smelt different, even more whiffy. To chase they were just the same. I've never caught any, not one in all my life, but they're such fun to chase.

I stayed quite close to Dorothy and Scarecrow. I didn't want to get too close to the Tin Woodman. He was clanking along quite clumsily, still not used to walking, I could tell that.

He was all arms and legs, walking a bit like a puppet on a string. I didn't want to get under his feet.

But it turned out to be very lucky that he was with us, because it wasn't very long before the yellow brick road had narrowed and the trees had grown so thick on either side that the branches blocked the way. Dorothy and I sat down, not knowing quite what to do.

But Tin Woodman chopped a way through for us, singing as he did so in time with his chopping. He was never jollier, I discovered, than when he was chopping.

I'm telling you, my little puppies, Tin Woodman could chop even better than Uncle Henry, and Uncle Henry is pretty darned handy with that axe of his. I mean, the yellow brick road had been grown right over by the forest on either side. We would never have got through without the tin woodman and his axe, so we were mighty pleased to have him along.

Once a way through was cleared, Dorothy clapped her hands and we all got ready to be on our way again. "Up we get and off we go!" she said. "Off down the yellow brick road!"

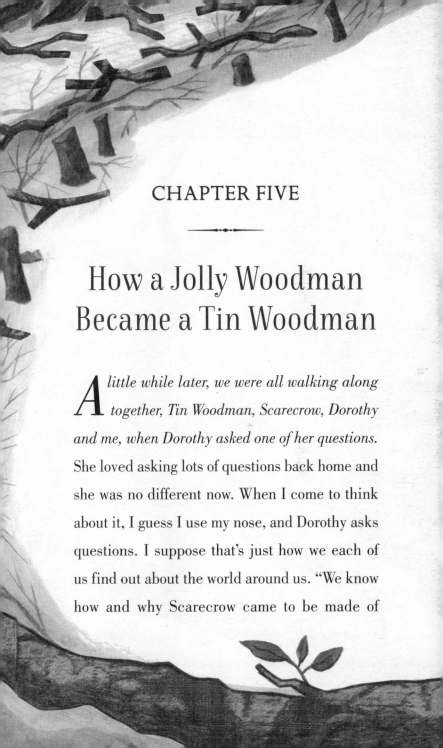

CHAPTER FIVE

How a Jolly Woodman Became a Tin Woodman

A little while later, we were all walking along together, Tin Woodman, Scarecrow, Dorothy and me, when Dorothy asked one of her questions. She loved asking lots of questions back home and she was no different now. When I come to think about it, I guess I use my nose, and Dorothy asks questions. I suppose that's just how we each of us find out about the world around us. "We know how and why Scarecrow came to be made of straw," she began. "But how come you're made of tin, if you don't mind my asking?"

"Not at all," replied Tin Woodman. "I wasn't like this always you know. I was a regular sort of a woodman, like my pa, a forester. We lived in that cottage in the woods, Pa, Ma and me. Life was hard, but life was good. We kept ourselves warm through the long winters, always had just about enough to eat. That forest provided all we needed. Then one sad day a tree fell on Pa, as he was cutting it down, and he died. I looked after Ma after that, till she died too a few years later, and then I was all alone. You know something, you never know what lonely is till you are really alone, alone all day, alone all night, with no one to talk to. I talked to myself a fair bit, sang when I worked, just to keep myself from getting too sad. But I was sad.

"Then one day I got lucky. I was taking my wood to the charcoal burner in the forest, when I met his daughter, Angelina, who had just begun to work with him, and she smiled at me and I smiled at her. That's how these things often get started. Well, soon enough the two of us had decided we wanted to marry and be together. Her father was fine about it, but her mother took against me, said her daughter deserved better than me, a man from the town with some money and good prospects, not a poor woodman who lived in the forest and chopped wood all day.

"Well, we told her we were going to get married whether she liked it or not. Do you know what that mother of hers did? She went to the Wicked Witch of the East and made a deal. She told the Wicked Witch she would give her two sheep and a cow if she would somehow stop the two of us getting married. And the Wicked Witch of the East – who was, if you didn't know it, just about the wickedest witch there ever has been in all the world – she put a spell on my axe, without me knowing, of course.

"I thought I was just being clumsy when the accidents began to happen. I was out in the forest one day, chopping wood as usual, when the axe slipped out of my hand and cut off my left leg.

Well, what was I to do? If I was going to marry Angelina, I needed to set myself up, and build a proper house for us. I needed to keep working. So I went to the tin-smith in town, and got him to make me another leg. It was a perfect fit, almost as good as the one I had had before. I could work again. But the next time I went out chopping, my axe slipped again and I chopped off the other leg.

"Well, I wasn't going to give up, was I? I got the tin-smith to make me another new leg. Back to work I went. But that axe of mine seemed to have a mind of its own, and I had accident after accident. I lost one arm, then the other, and then I lost my head too, cut it right off. But every time the tin-smith mended me, new tin arms to go with the legs, a new tin head, I thought nothing could go wrong now. But then that cursed axe slipped again, and cut me in two, cut the heart right out of me. The tin-smith saved me yet again, gave me all the joints I needed, so I could move about, move everything just as well as before – well, almost. It's amazing what people can do these days. 'Just keep them well oiled,' he said, 'and you'll be fine.' But the tin-smith also told me he couldn't make a heart of tin, that my body would always be hollow. I would be empty inside – there was nothing he could do about that.

"Angelina still loved me well enough, even though I was all made of tin now, but when I told her I had no heart inside me, that was more than she could bear, and her love for me died. Maybe I should never have told her, but I reckon you have to be honest and true with those you love. There was many a day afterwards when I wished I had never told her. After we parted, I didn't just feel empty inside, my whole life seemed empty."

I was thinking then about what it would be like to lose Dorothy. Just the thought of it made me feel awfully sad and empty inside.

"I never thought I would," went on Tin Woodman, "but in time I got over it, and became quite happy with my new clanky tin body. It shone in the sun and everyone noticed me in town. Everyone heard me coming, and I liked clanking about. When I danced it made everyone laugh. That's what got rid of my sadness: laughter, other folk's laughter. I learnt to laugh again. Now I was Jolly Woodman once more to my friends – and with a difference: I was Jolly Tin Woodman. I liked being different. I was proud of being different. And, what's more, I sang better now that I was tin, my voice booming louder. I liked to hear it echoing out through the forest as I worked. It didn't matter if my axe slipped any more. It couldn't hurt me now. It just clanked and bounced off.

"There was only one problem, I discovered. My joints. If ever I got wet, they would stiffen up and rust. So I knew I had to keep an oil can handy all the time, which I did. But then one day I forgot it, left it in the cottage by mistake one morning when I went off to work, and I was caught in a sudden thunderstorm. I don't like to be out there in the open

when there's lightning about. Lightning likes tin, did you know that? I don't know what it is, but if there's lightning about, it seems to want to seek me out. And if it strikes me, and it has too, well, it hurts – my, how it hurts. It burns me, scorches me.

"I wanted to run home, to get my oil can, but I didn't dare. I stayed under the trees and just got wet, dripping wet.

"And the storm raged on and on, rained cats and dogs it did. Anyway, it wasn't long before my joints stiffened up, and then they rusted, neck first, shoulders, hips, knees, ankles, and soon I couldn't move at all. So that's how come you found me a year and more later, stiff as a poker, and all rusted up. But standing there for so long gave me time to think. You have to keep hoping, I told myself, hoping and dreaming. It was my dream and my hope to have a heart again one day, and then you came along, my dear new friends, and now I'm off to see the Great Wizard of Oz to ask him for a new heart. Won't a new heart be wonderful?"

"Not as wonderful as brains," Scarecrow told him. "Brains are more useful than a heart, for a fool like me would not even know what to do with his heart. Give me brains any time."

"But I promise you, Scarecrow," said Tin Woodman,

"brains cannot make you happy, not without a heart. And happiness is the most wonderful, most important thing in the whole wide world."

But I was thinking not of hearts or of brains but of sausages. Happiness for me was sausages.

To be honest, I didn't much care which it was better to have, brains or a heart. I was hungry. And I think Dorothy felt the same, though she didn't say so. All she had in her basket now, besides Uncle Henry's hat, was that oil can. No sandwiches, no fruit, no nothing.

"We've got to find some food from somewhere, Toto," she said. I've often noticed that Dorothy and me, we often seem to be thinking the same thing at the same time.

I think it's because we know each other so well, and that's because we love each other so much.

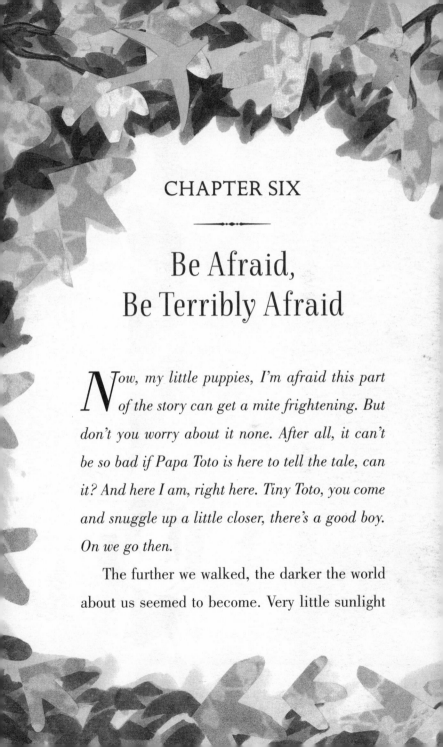

CHAPTER SIX

Be Afraid, Be Terribly Afraid

*N*ow, my little puppies, I'm afraid this part of the story can get a mite frightening. But don't you worry about it none. After all, it can't be so bad if Papa Toto is here to tell the tale, can it? And here I am, right here. Tiny Toto, you come and snuggle up a little closer, there's a good boy. On we go then.

The further we walked, the darker the world about us seemed to become. Very little sunlight found its way through because the trees grew so tall and thick on either side of the yellow brick road. Well, you couldn't hardly call it yellow any more. The road, what little you could see of it, was covered in leaves and branches and twigs. If there were any birds about, they had stopped singing. The quietness of the forest was eerie, and I was glad of Tin Woodman's clanking steps, and his cheery singing and humming. He kept my spirits up, but I needed more than a song to keep me going. I kept looking up at Dorothy with my eyes, telling her what I was after. "Food, I need food," I was trying to say. "Anything will do, anything. How about one of these?" I picked up a nut from the road to show her.

"Hazelnuts!" she cried, bending down to gather all she could. Tin Woodman and Scarecrow helped her, and soon there was a whole pile of them. "We have to crack them open," said Dorothy. "Tin Woodman, would you be very kind and stamp on these for us? Toto and me, we are so hungry."

"Easily done," he replied, and with one stamp he

cracked them all. So Dorothy and I feasted ourselves on all the nuts we could eat. It wasn't much, but it was a lot better than nothing. Neither Tin Woodman nor Scarecrow wanted any of them – eating just didn't seem to interest them. So the nuts were all for us. Dorothy filled her basket with all the hazelnuts and chestnuts and walnuts she could find, and on we went, much happier now, both of us. I was trotting on, and she was skipping along, and singing too. Tin Woodman and Scarecrow joined in after a while. Strange sound they made together, but they seemed to like it. Life was good again, despite the shadowy gloom and the mizzly mist all about us. But soon enough the singing stopped, the skipping and trotting slowed to a walk, then a weary plodding.

"My feet ache. My legs ache," Dorothy said. "I don't like to complain – Aunt Em said I shouldn't – but how far is it to the Emerald City, do you know, Tin Woodman?"

"I have no idea," he said, stomping on, and clanking

loudly as he went. "My pa went there once. I don't like to frighten you, but I remember he did say this was dangerous country to travel through, so it's a good thing there are four of us. We can all look after each other, can't we? I'm not afraid, so long as you look after that oil can, Dorothy. Scarecrow doesn't have a brain, so he can't be scared. You have to have a brain to be scared."

"Fire," said Scarecrow. "I don't like fire at all. I'm not scared of it, I just don't like it. And Dorothy told me she was once kissed by the Good Witch of the North, so no one can harm her. So she's got nothing to be scared of. That only leaves Toto. Do you think Toto is frightened?"

I growled at that, just to show everyone I was scared of nothing and no one, which wasn't true of course, but none of them were to know that, except Dorothy, who knew everything about me.

"Toto may be small, but he's very brave…" said Dorothy, "…well, mostly. We can all look after Toto, can't we? That's what friends are for, isn't it? Nothing and no one will ever hurt you, Toto. Promise."

It was just as Dorothy said these last words that we heard a terrible roaring from the forest, and before we had time even to run, a huge lion leapt out of the trees right in front of us. "Be afraid," he roared, "be terribly afraid."

In a trice, the lion lashed out with his paw and Scarecrow was sent flying. And then he did the same thing to Tin Woodman, sending him sprawling on the road with much clattering and crashing. Then the lion turned on Dorothy, and roared mightily. Until now, I had just stood there too shocked to move, but I didn't at all like the way he was looking at Dorothy, so I went for him, charged at him, making like I was a wolf, barking wildly, tail pointing, back bristling like a bottle brush. No one threatens my Dorothy. I'd show him!

That was when the lion rounded on me, and opened his great mouth and roared at me with all his sharp white teeth, with all his horrible bad breath. Any moment I knew I'd be a dead dog. But then Dorothy

rushed forward and gave him a big push and slapped him on his paw.

"Naughty, naughty lion," she was shouting. "Don't you dare bite my dear little Toto. How could you? You should be ashamed of yourself, a great big lion like you attacking a sweet little dog. You nasty, nasty lion. Put your claws away this minute." I don't think I had ever seen Dorothy so furious. To my amazement, the lion did not attack her or me, but shrank back, whining pitifully and rubbing his nose with the side of his paw.

"You didn't have to push me," the lion cried – and he was crying, really crying. "I wasn't going to bite him."

"But you were trying to, weren't you?" Dorothy said. "You're a bad, bad lion. Look how small little Toto is, and how big and strong you are. You're just a big horrible bully, and a coward too, what's more. And what did Scarecrow ever do to you, or Tin Woodman? Why did you need to knock them about like that? How could they hurt you? One is made of nothing but straw, the other of nothing but tin. And they're nice, kind folk, too, and they're my friends. You're a cowardy, cowardy custard, that's what you are."

I was still barking at him for all I was worth, so that the lion should know I was agreeing with everything Dorothy was telling him. The lion sat back and put his paws over his ears. "Don't be so angry with me," he said. "You frighten me so."

"How can you be frightened of little Toto?" Dorothy asked him. "I mean, look at him. He's so small and sweet. And you're a ginormous, humongous lion! You're supposed to be the king of beasts! And you really are a coward, aren't you?"

"I think I must be the most cowardly lion that ever lived," the lion said sadly. "I can roar. I can bare my teeth, but at heart I'm just a softie. Even when I'm out

hunting, a deer only has to stamp her foot at me and I run. That's why I go hungry a lot. I have always been like this, and it makes me so sad, so unhappy. I know a lion is supposed to be brave. My mother and my father brought me up to be like that, but I'm not. I think I was born like this, with no courage inside me. You mustn't ever tell anyone, but I am useless as a lion, not one ounce of courage in my whole miserable body." And then the lion was weeping so piteously that I stopped barking and Dorothy went to put an arm round him to comfort him.

"Have you got any brains, Lion?" Scarecrow asked him.

"I think so," the lion replied. "Why do you ask?"

"Because I have no brains at all," Scarecrow said. "My head has no room for a brain, it is stuffed with straw. I'm going to the Great and Terrible Wizard of Oz in the Emerald City to ask him to give me some brains, so I can think."

"And I am going to ask him for a heart," said the

Tin Woodman, "so I can feel again, like I used to before I was just tin."

"And I'm going to ask him if he can tell Toto and me how to get back home to Kansas," said Dorothy. "Home is home, and home is best."

"You're so dog-gone right," I woofed.

"So, might I ask him for some courage, do you think?" asked Lion. "Would he do that for me? Then I could be a proper lion."

"Why not?" said Dorothy. "Come along with us, Lion. Just so long as you don't eat us, we'd be more than glad to have you, wouldn't we? You can help Toto frighten away anyone who tries to hurt us on the way. Would you do that for us?"

"Of course," said Lion, wiping away the last of his tears. "I shall pretend to be the bravest lion there ever was. Like this." And with that he roared so loudly, and bared his teeth so horribly, that we forgot for several moments that he was just pretending.

So now there were five of us – Dorothy, Scarecrow, Tin Woodman, Lion and me – off to see the Great and Terrible Wizard of Oz. They all seemed to think he was a wonderful and wise wizard, Dorothy too, but I wasn't so sure. He sounded a bit scary to me. I mean, he wasn't called "terrible" for nothing, was he?

And talking of scary, Lion loped along beside us, not scary any more at all, but as friendly as you like. I liked him. I so wanted to be big and strong like him, with a roar that terrified the world. And he liked me too. "Toto, my friend," he said as we walked along, "you may be small, with little legs and little teeth, but you stood up to me to protect Dorothy. You have the courage of a lion already, a proper lion."

But if I'm honest, from time to time when he looked down at me, licking his whiskery lips and showing me his great teeth, I couldn't make up my mind whether he was smiling at me or thinking of me as his next meal. Lion may not have been brave, but he was clever. He seemed to know what I was thinking. "I'd never eat you, little Toto," he said, "nor Dorothy, nor Tin Woodman, nor Scarecrow, because you are my friends. I like you too much. And besides, I have decided none of you would taste very nice. I'm most particular about what I eat, I can tell you." I was much relieved and very pleased indeed to hear it.

Friendly though I was now with Lion, I liked above all to be alone with Dorothy. She would tell me all her hopes and fears, and I would listen, or at least pretend to. Often we would find ourselves walking ahead together, Lion and Scarecrow and Tin Woodman far behind us.

"I like our new friends, Toto," she told me once, "but every night I dream of Kansas and home and Aunt Em and Uncle Henry. Do you think they are all right? Won't it be nice to go home? I'm not complaining, mind. I have lovely new red shoes, three new friends, and you, Toto. I have you, my best friend in all the world." She looked over her shoulder, and went on in a whisper. "They are strange companions, Toto, aren't they? I mean, did you see how upset Tin Woodman was when he stepped on that beetle and squashed it by mistake? Cried his eyes out, didn't he? He had tears running down his face. Did you see? I had to wipe them away, and then oil his jaw so it didn't rust up again. He was so sad. Well, you can't be sad if you haven't got a heart, can you?"

I told her with my eyes that I agreed, that I didn't know what they were all fussing about so much. It seemed to me too that Scarecrow wasn't brainless at all,

he just thought he was. And I wouldn't have minded betting either that deep down Lion was as brave as any other lion in the world.

I told her something else with my eyes too, and my tail. "I'm so hungry," I told her. "I could do with a sausage or two!"

"Me too," she said.

CHAPTER SEVEN

Lost in the Forest of the Cruel Kalidahs

Well, I can tell you this for sure, little puppies, everyone was mighty glad to have Lion with us after that, because every mile we walked on down the yellow brick road, the forest around us grew thicker and darker and scarier. Lion would let out a dreadful roar from time to time just to warn off anyone or anything that might be lurking in the forest that night, which might spring out suddenly and attack us. We'd left the Munchkins and their lovely countryside well behind us by now. There were no kind Munchkins to take us in and give us shelter and food, so that night for the first time we had to camp out. Tin Woodman chopped up enough wood to make a blazing fire, so at least we were warm, and Lion insisted a good fire would keep all the wild animals away, but that we had to keep it going, and keep the flames crackling. "Even the cruel Kalidahs don't like fire," he said.

"What are Kalidahs?" Dorothy asked.

"You don't need to know," Lion replied in a whisper, looking around him nervously. "And I don't want to talk about them. They frighten me silly." He lifted his head and sniffed the air. "I am rather hungry. I smell deer. I think I shall go and catch my dinner."

"Oh, please don't kill a deer," cried Tin Woodman, "I couldn't bear it. I shall cry if you do, then my jaw will rust again."

Lion said no more about it, but kept licking his lips at the thought of a meal, which only reminded me of how hungry I was. "If we go to sleep, Toto," Dorothy said, as we lay down together near the warmth of the fire, "then we won't feel hungry any more." That sounded like sense, but I knew it wasn't true. Once I am hungry, I am hungry even in my dreams. I have had more sausage dreams than hot dinners – if you see what I am saying.

Scarecrow was so kind to us. Even though he didn't like coming anywhere near the fire, he brought armfuls of dry leaves to cover Dorothy and me as we lay there.

"Sleep tight," he said, and then went to stand guard with Tin Woodman at a safe distance from the fire. Lion snored us to sleep, and by the time we woke the next morning Scarecrow and Tin Woodman had collected a pile of nuts for our breakfast, and cracked them open too. I had never much liked nuts until now, but perhaps I had never been so hungry as I was that morning. Dorothy and I wolfed some down – so to speak – while Tin Woodman and Scarecrow filled the basket with more nuts.

Dorothy oiled Tin Woodman's joints to make him feel looser after all the damp dew of the morning, and off we went on our way.

It wasn't long before we came to a great chasm that cut right across the road. The forest was impenetrable on both sides – impenetrable, in case you don't know, means the forest was so thick you couldn't find a way through it. Sometimes, little puppies, long words are best, and it makes me feel good to use them. Anyway, all you need to know is that there was no way for us to go. We stood on the edge of the great wide chasm and looked down, which made me feel a bit sick. It was too steep to climb down on our side, and too steep to climb up on the other side.

"Now what?" asked Tin Woodman.

We all thought about it for a long time. It seemed hopeless.

"Well, I think," Scarecrow began slowly, "I think this. We can't fly over, can we? So logically, either we shall have to stop and stay where we are, or we'll just have to jump it. Nothing else for it."

"How clever you are to think of that," said Dorothy. And Scarecrow looked suddenly so pleased with himself, and so happy.

Lion said then: "I'm a pretty good jumper, though I say it myself. I could jump this chasm – I think."

"And when you jump, Lion, do you think you could carry us over on your back, one by one?" asked Scarecrow.

"I could try," Lion replied, trying his very best to sound brave. "But you'll all have to hold on very tight to my mane," he went on. "You first perhaps, Scarecrow. You're made of straw, aren't you? So you must be the lightest. If I can't jump across with you on my back then I can hardly do it with anyone heavier, can I? Up you get, Scarecrow. Let's go for it before I can change my mind. You ready? Hang on!"

Then to everyone's amazement, mine too, Lion didn't do a running jump. He just loped up to the edge of the chasm, stopped for a moment or two, and then, as if he had springs in his legs, just took a great leap and landed easily on the other side.

"How did you do that?" Scarecrow gasped.

"Springing is what lions do," Lion said, and as if to prove it, he sprang back over at once to fetch Tin Woodman, who climbed on his back and clung so tight that Lion had to ask him to loosen his grip because he couldn't breathe. When they landed on the other side, Tin Woodman fell off with quite a clang and a crash. But he was soon up on his feet and waving across at us quite happily. All was well. Then it was our turn. Somehow Dorothy managed to hold me tight and hang on to Lion's mane at the same time.

For a moment, as Lion leapt over the gaping chasm below us, it seemed as if we were really flying! By the time we landed I had my eyes closed. We were all safely across!

Dorothy said what we were all thinking. "How brave you were to do that, Lion!" And Lion looked suddenly so pleased with himself, and so happy.

But our troubles were not over. On the other side of the chasm, the forest was even darker still. Even though it was still morning, the sky was almost as black as night. The yellow brick road led on ahead of us, our only comfort in the gloom around us. Lion lifted his head to scent the air. So I did too. I didn't like what I smelt, didn't like it at all, but I didn't know what it was.

"I smell Kalidahs," whispered Lion. "They are near, and they are many. Walk softly, as softly as you can." Tin Woodman did his best, walking on tiptoe. He clanked softer now, but he still clanked. He couldn't help himself.

"What are they like, these cruel Kalidahs?" Dorothy asked.

"I don't think you want to know," whispered Lion, looking about him anxiously.

"I do," said Dorothy.

"Well then," Lion said, "since you ask. They have heads like tigers, bodies like bears and claws as sharp as… I don't want to think about their claws. Believe me, you never want to meet a Kalidah. If they hear us, we are done for. We must all be as quiet as mice."

"I'm doing my best," said Tin Woodman. "But it's not easy being tin, you know." Then, quite unexpectedly, and most unfortunately, the yellow brick road seemed simply to stop. It began again further on, but on the far side of a deep black hole in the road.

"Oh no!" cried Dorothy. "It's another chasm, like the last one, only wider and deeper. We'll never be able to jump this one."

Lion agreed. He stood there on the edge of the black hole, shaking his head. "I'd have to be a kangaroo to jump this," he said, "and I'm not."

Scarecrow was standing beside Lion, scratching his head, which he always seemed to do when he was thinking. "Tell you what. I have an idea," he said. "You see that big tree over there? Now if Tin Woodman could cut it down for us so that it fell right across, then we could walk over, couldn't we? Simple." We all looked at Scarecrow in utter disbelief.

"What a great idea!" Dorothy said.

"Not a great idea," Scarecrow told her, "just a simple one. I haven't any brains, but I do have simple ideas from time to time."

"I don't think you're simple at all," said Dorothy.

"Hurry," said Lion, lifting his nose and scenting the air again. "The Kalidahs are close." I lifted my nose too.

Rotten eggs! If these Kalidahs smelt like rotten eggs, then they were very close indeed.

So Tin Woodman got to work right away chopping down the tree, and soon it was toppling across the ravine, falling with a huge crash and making just the bridge we needed. One by one we ran over, trying very hard not to look down. I was almost across with Dorothy and Scarecrow, but Tin Woodman and Lion were behind us and only halfway over when we all heard a terrible snarling and growling. Out of the trees they came, charging towards the bridge, towards us, two ferocious-looking Kalidahs. Monstrous they were, half tiger, half bear.

"Get across," cried Lion, turning to face them and roaring his defiance. "I shall stay here and fight them off. Go. Go. I won't let them pass. Don't worry. Go!" So we did as he said and ran for it until we were all safely across. When we looked, we saw Lion was still there on the tree trunk over the black hole, roaring his worst, flashing his claws, shaking his mane, baring his teeth. But I could see, we all could, that the Kalidahs were coming closer all the time, about to pounce on him. There were two of them, and one of him, and they were each twice his size, with claws as big and sharp as Uncle Henry's scythes back home in Kansas.

Suddenly Tin Woodman had his axe in his hand and

was chopping away at the branches of the tree on our side of the black hole. "Lion!" cried Tin Woodman as he chopped. "Listen to me, Lion. I shall chop six more times and then the tree will fall down into the ravine. On the fifth chop, turn and run back to us as fast as you can. You hear me?"

"I hear you," cried Lion. "I am not that good at counting, but I will do my best! Keep chopping." One chop, two, three, and everyone was counting out loud now to help Lion, me too. The Kalidahs were almost on him, and he was still roaring at them.

Four.

Five…

"Run, Lion! Run!" we all shouted. Lion turned and raced back along the bridge.

Six!

The tree was shaking, slipping, falling. At the very last moment Lion leapt to safety.

Down into the rocky depths of the black hole went the tree, and those dreadful Kalidahs with it. Lion took a deep breath. "My poor heart is pounding with fear.

I thought we were done for, but it seems we shall all live a little longer after all."

"I rather like that idea," said Scarecrow. "To live a little longer, I mean. With or without brains, I don't think I should like not to be alive." And Dorothy clapped her hands and told them all how wonderfully clever and brave they had been, and I barked and barked till my head ached with it, telling them exactly the same thing.

It's a funny thing, but I reckon that fight with those horrible Kalidah creatures turned out to be just about the best thing that could have happened to us. After that, we all felt like one big family. True, a strange sort of family. Every one of us was mighty different from the other, about as different as we could be, but we all knew that if we stuck together everything would turn out just fine. Together we had beaten the Kalidahs, together we would reach the Emerald City, whatever dangers we might have to face on the way. We would face them together.

Lion and I padded along together ahead of the others, the best of friends, on the lookout for trouble, and behind us came the rest, arm in arm, sometimes singing as they went, Tin Woodman's great feet clanking on the yellow brick road. There never was a happier band, except for two things – I was getting mighty fed up by this time with eating nothing but nuts, and Dorothy's singing wasn't getting any better either.

CHAPTER EIGHT

One Bad Situation After Another

*W**e all thought nothing could ever be more dangerous than the cruel Kalidahs.* But none of us had reckoned with poppies. Yes, poppies, little puppies, I am not kidding you. And first we had to cross a raging river and rescue poor Scarecrow, which wasn't easy either. But I'm getting ahead of myself, aren't I? Mustn't do that. Now where was I? Oh yes.

Things were looking pretty good. We followed

the yellow brick road for quite a while and it led us gradually, gradually, out of the dark of the forest and into bright sunlight and grassy flowery meadows with singing birds and fruit trees humming with bees. There was lots of fruit to eat now, plums, pears, peaches, all we wanted – all Dorothy wanted anyway; she's crazy about fruit. It was better than nuts, made a change at least, but Lion and me, we had hunting on our minds. There were rabbits everywhere now, and deer flitting through the trees. Dorothy didn't like me catching rabbits, and Tin Woodman and Scarecrow would have been very sad if Lion had brought back a deer to eat. Both of us knew that, so both of us ate fruit and had to be happy with it, but whenever I lay down to sleep I dreamed of rabbits – rabbits for me were almost as good as sausages. And Lion dreamed of deer – he told me so.

For days and days we walked on down the yellow brick road, until one morning we came to a rushing river, with no bridge across it, not that we could see anyway. We just had to get over it somehow. There on the other side the yellow brick road began again, the road that would take us to the Emerald City and the Great Wizard of Oz. "How are we ever going to cross this?" Dorothy said, shaking her head. "Toto can swim, but I can't."

Scarecrow scratched his head for a moment or two, and we knew then that he was going to come up with one of his brilliant ideas. "Simple," he said, "a no-brainer. A raft. Tin Woodman cuts down a tree or two and we build a raft."

So that's what we all did, and that was how we came to find ourselves a while later floating across the river, Tin Woodman and Scarecrow each with a long pole, pushing us, guiding us towards the far bank. But we soon realised we were in trouble. We weren't floating across the river – we were being carried down it. Scarecrow and Tin Woodman were doing their best with their poles, pushing with all their might, but it was no use. The current was sweeping us downstream, and the river was running faster and faster all the time, swirling us around and around.

"Oh no," cried Tin Woodman, "we shall end up in the river, or, worse still, in the land of the Wicked Witch of the West, and she's just like the Wicked Witch of the East was before you squashed her, Dorothy. She makes bad magic. There never was a wickeder witch. She'll make us her slaves. Then we'll never get to see the Great Wizard of Oz, and I'll never have a new heart."

"And I will never have the courage I should have," said Lion.

"And I will never have any brains," said Scarecrow. "We have to push harder, Tin Woodman, as hard as we can!" And with that Scarecrow plunged his pole deep into the river, down into the mud, and pushed with all his might. But there it stuck fast. Scarecrow should have let go of his pole, but he didn't, he wouldn't. So he found himself clinging on to the pole in the middle of the swirling river, watching us drift further and further away from him on the raft.

"We have to save him!" Dorothy cried.

"First we have to save ourselves," said Lion. "I shall swim for the bank. Tin Woodman, you hang on to the tip of my tail. I will dive in and pull the raft across. Whatever you do, don't let go of my tail."

So Tin Woodman grabbed his tail. And in Lion jumped. I could see at once he needed some help. I barked at Dorothy and she understood right away.

If Lion can swim in that swirling river, I thought, *then so can I.*

Dorothy knelt down on the edge of the raft, grabbed my tail, and in I jumped after Lion. Soon I was paddling for the shore like crazy alongside him. I was getting pretty puffed out, I can tell you, but somehow we made it across the river in the end, towing that raft, with Dorothy and Tin Woodman on board, all the way. Our troubles were by no means over though. We may have reached the other side, but we had drifted a long way downstream by now. There was no sign of poor Scarecrow clinging to his pole in the middle of the river, no sign either of the yellow brick road. It was not a good situation.

"We have to find Scarecrow and rescue him!" cried Dorothy. "We can't go on without Scarecrow, we just can't."

"Well, there's only one thing to be done," said Lion, who was shaking himself dry in the sun, showering us all, and somehow making at the same time a great rainbow around his mane and head, like a rainbow crown it was. "If we walk back along the river," he went on, "we should soon find him, and the yellow brick road as well."

I shook myself dry, hoping to make a rainbow too, but I didn't because I didn't have a mane. I so wanted to be like Lion, be brave like him, roar like him, have teeth as big as him, make rainbows like him. When he bounded off along the riverbank, I followed him. We all did, all of us worrying we might be too late, that Scarecrow might already have been swept away.

As we came round a bend in the river, I saw him first.

"Help!" Scarecrow was crying. "Help me, please. I can't hold on much longer."

He was slipping down the pole, his feet already almost in the water. All of us looked at one another. There was nothing we could do to save him. He was too far away, the river was running too fast, we were too late.

Just then, the most wonderful thing happened. Floating down on his great wide, white wings, there came a stork. He landed right beside us on the riverbank. "You all seem rather upset," he said. "Is there anything I can do?"

"Our dear friend Scarecrow," Dorothy explained. "He's stuck out there in the river on that pole, and we can't help him."

"Scarecrow, you say?" the stork said. "We birds don't usually like scarecrows. But he looks like a nice sort of a scarecrow, so I'll rescue him for you if that is what you'd like. He's only made of straw. He shouldn't

be too heavy. Come on, wings! Do your thing. Off I go, up up up and away!"

The stork lifted off and with a few strong beats of his wings he was hovering out over the pole in the middle of the river.

He grasped Scarecrow by his arm, then carried him back, setting him down gently in amongst us.

I never in my life saw so much hugging. Tin Woodman cried and Dorothy had to dry his tears quickly, oiling him again, before his jaw went stiff on him. I leapt up into Dorothy's arms and joined in all the hugging, only I do licking a lot better than hugging.

Lion was up on his hind legs, his huge paws on Tin Woodman's shoulders, smiling toothily, very toothily.

Luckily he had his claws hidden away else he would have scratched Tin Woodman all over.

The stork hopped up and down, cackling all the while. "I like to make people happy," he cried. "But I must go now. There are babies waiting for me in my nest. So long, you guys. Be happy."

"We are, we will be," cried Dorothy. "Thank you ever, ever, ever so much."

Off he flew, and Dorothy clapped her hands. "Let's not waste time!" she cried. "Up we get and off we go!"

I woofed, and the others laughed. They loved me woofing.

On we went along the river, Scarecrow arm in arm with Tin Woodman and Dorothy, all of us smiling, all of us searching for the yellow brick road. This was the most beautiful countryside we had been through, brilliantly coloured flowers and butterflies and birds wherever we looked. We were all so happy, happy to be together again, and on the right side of the river.

So when we saw the field of red poppies on the hillside ahead of us, and beyond it the yellow brick road, we cheered and barked and roared and clapped and clanked, all of it with joy. Never had we seen a prettier sight! All we had to do was cross that poppy field and we'd be on our way again to the Emerald City and to the Great and Terrible Wizard of Oz.

Head-high the poppies were for me as we walked up over the hillside. Dorothy kept rubbing her eyes and yawning as she went (which I thought was rather odd).

She was obviously quite sleepy, and then suddenly I was too. And Lion was as well (which I also thought was rather odd).

He was yawning – I never saw so many teeth in all my life! But I was too tired to care. When Dorothy lay down to sleep, I lay down beside her.

Tin Woodman kept trying to shake us, to wake us

up, to help us back on to our feet. "You mustn't go to sleep. You mustn't. It's the poppies making you sleep. You go to sleep now, you'll never wake up! Up, on your feet! We have to walk on!" he was shouting at us, shaking us.

But my eyes felt heavy. I could hardly keep them open. Everything began to go dark.

"I like poppies," I heard Lion murmuring. He was lying down right beside me, but his voice seemed far, far away, as if in some dream. "Toto and Dorothy are falling asleep, so I will too. I'll have a nice long sleep. I think I could sleep for ever."

"Up, up, Lion!" cried Scarecrow. "On your feet!" And he was pushing at Lion with all his might, shaking him and shaking him. Tin Woodman was helping him too. "It's the poppies, they're making you sleepy. We have to get out of this poppy field before it's too late. Tin Woodman and me, we can carry Dorothy and Toto.

But we cannot carry you, Lion. You are too heavy for us."

"Don't you feel sleepy too?" murmured Lion.

"The scent of the poppies cannot affect us," said Tin Woodman. "There are some advantages to being made of straw and tin. Please get up, Lion, please!"

I felt myself being lifted up and carried then. I don't know if it was Tin Woodman or Scarecrow who got me out of there. But get us out they did, me and Dorothy both. All I know is that when we woke some time later, we were lying in soft grass by the river, a gentle breeze wafting us awake. Tin Woodman was there kneeling over us, Scarecrow too. But when I woke up properly and I looked around, there was no sign of Lion anywhere.

"Where is Lion?" Dorothy asked, sitting up. "What's happened to him?"

"He is lying out there in the field of poppies, fast asleep," said Scarecrow sadly. "But he won't last long, I'm afraid. Stay there in amongst those deadly poppies and you never wake up."

"We couldn't carry him out, Dorothy," Tin Woodman told her. "Lion is too heavy. Scarecrow and me, we tried and we tried. We couldn't move him. We may not be seeing Lion again, I'm afraid. I'm so sorry, Dorothy."

CHAPTER NINE

———◆———

How Lion was Saved by a Mouse – or Two

*D*on't go getting yourselves all upset now, little puppies. Things are never as bad as how they seem. Lion is going to be all right, you'll see. You just listen up and you'll hear how it happened.

We were lost. We were still looking for the yellow brick road, and couldn't find it, when we saw this great tawny wildcat come a-bounding towards us, a-snorting and a-spitting like wildcats do. But he wasn't after us. He was chasing a little

grey field mouse who wasn't doing him any harm. Well, I don't like cats, never have done, wildcat or not. That wildcat was mighty big, and the little grey field mouse, he was, well… little, as well as being kind of cute too, so I reckoned that wasn't fair. And, besides, I wanted to chase that mouse myself, which is why I started running and barking at that wildcat, telling him exactly what I thought of him.

He didn't hang around.

Wildcats don't like dogs any more than we like them. Difference is, they're plum scared of us dogs, and if I'm honest I don't think he much liked the look of the fearsome axe that Tin Woodman was whirling about his head. That old wildcat, he took off and I went right after him. When I came back, the little mouse was hiding behind Tin Woodman's leg, all shivering and shaking he was.

"Is he gone?" he asked.

"You're safe now," said Tin Woodman, "thanks to Toto."

"How can I ever thank you?" said the mouse. "If there's ever anything I can do for you in return, you only have to ask."

"Isn't he sweet?" said Dorothy, crouching down beside the little field mouse.

"He? He?" squeaked the mouse. "I'm not a he! I'm a she, and I am not just any old mouse either. I'm Queen of all the field mice."

"Oh, I'm so sorry, Your Majesty," said Dorothy, and

bowed. Tin Woodman bowed. Scarecrow bowed. I didn't bow. Dogs don't bow to anyone.

At that moment, there was a scurrying of tiny feet and suddenly all around us were hundreds, thousands of mice, all of them leaping up and down and squeaking, so happy to see their queen was still alive. I'd never seen so many mice. Back home in Kansas, I'd have been after them at once, I can tell you that. I love a good mouse chase. I was sorely tempted. But, luckily for them, there were so many I couldn't make up my mind which one to chase and, before I could decide, Dorothy picked me up and was holding me tight.

"No, Toto," she whispered in my ear. "Don't spoil it. You've been a very good dog up until now. But I know you only chased off that big nasty wildcat because you wanted to chase the mouse for yourself. The others don't know that. They think you are a hero. I know you're just my lovely, naughty Toto!"

That's the whole darned thing about Dorothy: she knows me far too well.

Scarecrow was scratching his head again, so we all knew an idea must be coming, "S'cuse me, Mrs Queen," he began thoughtfully, "or Ma'am, or Your Majesty – never do know what to call queens – but you said that if ever there was anything you could do for us in return for Toto saving your life, just ask. Well, I'm asking. You see, our dear friend Lion is lying fast asleep over in that field of poppies, and if we don't get him out of there right now, he's going to sleep himself to death and never wake up. Trouble is, he's far too heavy for us to carry him out of there. We've tried. So I thought – Mrs Queen, Ma'am, Your Majesty, whatever – if all your thousands and thousands of field mice would lend us a helping hand, that we could, between us perhaps, manage to get him out of there and save him. He's a lovely lion. Wouldn't hurt a mouse, I promise you. I thought that if each one of your thousands of mice could find a little piece of string, or cotton or hair even, we could tie all of them together and make a strong rope; and then Tin Woodman here could cut us out some wheels and maybe make a cart big enough to carry him, and we could haul Lion out, and he could breathe good clean air and wake up and not die at all. What do you think?"

Everyone was speechless after this, simply gawping in amazement at Scarecrow; me too.

"Brilliant," cried Dorothy, clapping her hands in delight. "You're a genius, Scarecrow!"

And I woofed and woofed to tell him how clever I thought he was too.

"What's a genius?" Scarecrow asked, rather bewildered. "It's not a word I know. I'm not clever with words. No brains, you see." Everyone laughed at that, the mice too, and Scarecrow had no idea why. Then we all hurried away to carry out Scarecrow's master plan. The mice fetched all the little bits of string and cotton and hair from miles around and wound it all tight into a strong rope. Tin Woodman cut down a tree and made it into the four wheels we needed, then chopped and chopped until the cart itself was all made and ready.

"Ready to roll?" said Scarecrow. "Let's roll!"

All the field mice took hold of the rope, the mouse Queen and Dorothy and Tin Woodman too, as well as Scarecrow and me – I got it in my teeth – and we all of us pulled. We pulled and we pulled, and slowly, ever so slowly, the wheels began to turn and the cart moved, and off we went back to the field of poppies. There we found poor Lion lying fast asleep in amongst the flowers, snoring deeply. The longer we stayed in that deadly field, the more dangerous it was – we all knew that.

So we worked fast and we worked hard, all of us together, thousands of us, pulling and heaving, shoving and tugging, until at last we had hauled Lion up on to the cart.

It was nearly done. We still had to pull the cart out of the field as fast as we could. But I was beginning to feel drowsy again, so was Dorothy, so were the mice. Time was running out for every one of us, but, if we were going to save Lion, and save ourselves too, we had to do it.

So we just took hold of that rope again and we heaved. Yes, sir, we heaved that old cart out of that deadly field of poppies and into the sweetest, freshest air you ever did breathe. We breathed it in deep, coughing and spluttering, but we had done it, we had got him out of the poppy field.

Lion lay there, his eyes closed, and still, so still, too still.

"Breathe!" cried Dorothy. "You've got to take a breath!"

I had to do something. I licked his nose, his eyes, his ears. I woofed at him. He didn't move. Not a twitch.

"Oh no!" cried Dorothy. "Are we too late?"

Lion opened one eye.

"Oh!" he said. "I was having a very odd dream about mice." Then he saw the mice all around him. "Or maybe it wasn't a dream…"

Soon Lion was sitting up, and looking about, all sleepy still and bleary-eyed he was, and rubbing his face with his paws. We had saved him! He lay there now only half asleep in the back of the old cart, and we all joined hands and danced around him, singing for joy. Barking for joy in my case; I don't do singing.

"What's up?" he said. "What's all this singing? You woke me up."

"We did," cried Dorothy happily. "We did, didn't we?"

"Job done then," said the Queen of the field mice. "We'd better be going. Let us know if we can ever help you again, won't you?" And off they scampered.

"Thank you so much," Dorothy called after them.

"What are friends for?" came the faintest reply.

We waited a while down by the river for Lion to

wake up properly. "I had a funny dream," he told us. "There were lots of mice in it, and Tin Woodman was making a cart – I'm sure I don't know why…"

"We do, don't we?" Dorothy laughed. There was a whole lot of laughing as we walked on our way through the flowery meadows. Between them, Dorothy and Scarecrow and Tin Woodman told Lion everything that had happened.

"Well I never!" said Lion when they had finished. "That's so strange, because it's exactly what happened in my dream. Is that weird or what?"

On we walked, until we found the yellow brick road again, and soon after we began to notice that all the fences were green, emerald green, the houses too, and even the people wore green clothes and hats, not sky-blue like the Munchkins. They looked just like the Munchkins, sort of small and round, not blue though and not quite as friendly. They didn't smile much, nor whisper and chuckle amongst themselves like the Munchkins had.

It was evening time by now, and darkening. There were plenty of houses, plenty of faces at windows looking out at us, but no one invited us in, as the blue Munchkins had. So in the end Dorothy decided that if they wouldn't do it, we had to invite ourselves.

"We are tired out, right?" she said. "And we're hungry, right? Aunt Em always says you should invite strangers in, be hospitable. It's only good manners. Poor Toto hasn't had a proper meal for ages, have you, Toto?" She was right enough there! She marched up to a farmhouse door and knocked.

"What do you want?" came a woman's voice from inside.

"S'cuse me, ma'am," Dorothy began, "but we are awful tired and hungry. Can you help us, please?" The door opened just a little, and a face appeared. She was an old woman, rather thin and peaky-looking, with a green shawl round her shoulders. She eyed us all, looked us up and down.

"A lion, a dog, a tin man and a scarecrow, and a

girl," she said. "Does that dog bite?"

"No, ma'am."

"Does that lion eat people?"

"No, ma'am."

"And does that tin man and that scarecrow fella eat a lot? Cos we ain't got much."

"No, ma'am. They don't eat anything," said Dorothy. So the old woman opened the door. "Come along in then, and mind you wipe your feet. I only got porridge." The porridge was steaming hot and sweet with maple syrup, just how I like it best, just how Dorothy likes it too. Lion wasn't so keen. He wrinkled his nose at it.

"There's oats in there," he said. "Oats are for horses, not lions." So I ate his bowl too, every last lick of it.

"Well, Toto," said Dorothy to me. "That was just like Aunt Em's porridge, wasn't it? Just like home. Oh, home is home, and home is best, isn't it, Toto?"

"You're so dog-gone right," I woofed, licking my whiskers again.

"Where are you folks off to?" said the old woman, sitting down at the table with us when we had finished.

"We're going to the Emerald City to see the Great and Terrible Wizard of Oz," Dorothy told her.

"Are you indeed?" she said – she spoke rather croakily. "Well, that Emerald City is a fine and beautiful place all right, so bright and so beautiful it hurts your eyes to see it. But you won't see the Wizard of Oz. No one's ever seen him. No one even knows what he looks like. You hear different tales. Some say he looks like a bird, or a cat, or an elephant even. With just one click of his fingers, I heard, that old wizard can be just about whatever he wants to be. I mean, after all, he is all-powerful, isn't he?"

"Well, I wonder what he'll be when we meet him," said Dorothy.

"Don't you listen, girl?" snapped the old woman. "You won't meet him. No one does. Anyways, why in tarnation do you want to see him so much?"

So each of us told her why. She listened, nodding, and after a while thinking about it, she said: "He could do the heart, the brains and the courage, I reckon, but even the Great and Terrible Wizard of Oz could hardly get you and that dog of yours back to Kansas, not if he don't know where it is. I ain't ever heard of the place. Where in heck is Kansas?"

"It's somewhere," said Dorothy sadly. "I know it must be because Toto and me live there; it's our home."

"Well, just don't go counting on the Wizard of Oz for anything you want in this life," said the old woman. "That's all I can say. All I know is that if you want something bad enough, you got to go out and get it for yourself. And I got to warn you folks – cos you seem like nice enough people – that old Wizard of Oz can be mighty mean sometimes, that's what I heard."

Dorothy hugged me extra tight that night as we lay down by the old woman's fire. She kept whispering in my ear. "We will get home, Toto. Don't you worry, we will get to see Aunt Em and Uncle Henry again, whatever that old woman says."

CHAPTER TEN

———◆———

Face to Face with the Great and Terrible Wizard of Oz

*T*hree of you asleep already! I reckon there's some of you little puppies who still don't know the end of my tale. Never stayed awake that long, have you? And that's kind of a shame, because as Tiny Toto will tell you – and he never goes to sleep till it's over, do you, Tiny Toto? – he knows the end is just about the best bit. And getting to the end is the most exciting part, and the most frightening too, not frightening

enough to give you nightmares, but frightening
enough to be exciting. And we're coming right now
to the moment we met the Great and Terrible Wizard
of Oz, which was scary enough, I can tell you!

We were all up early the next morning. We said
our goodbyes and thanks to the old woman – who had
turned out not to be such a bad old stick after all – and
were soon off on our journey again, following the yellow
brick road. As the sun rose, we could see a green glow
in the sky.

"Look, it's the Emerald City!" cried Scarecrow.
"We're almost there!" And, linking arms with Tin
Woodman and Dorothy, off they all skipped ahead of
us, so that Lion and I had to trot along to keep up. As
we came ever closer, we saw the city was surrounded
by towering green walls, and set in the wall were great
green gates studded not with nails but with glittering
emeralds that dazzled our eyes. The gates swung open
as we approached and there stood the Guardian of the
gate, small and green like everyone in these parts,

but he wore an especially smart green uniform, with emerald buttons, and had a twirling green moustache that stretched across his face, from ear to ear. He stood before us, fingering his moustache.

"Yes?" he said. "And you are?"

He seemed rather an officious little man.

Dorothy explained very patiently and very politely who we were and that we'd come a very long way to see the Great and Terrible Wizard of Oz and how she would be very obliged if he would take us to see him.

"You do know," said the Guardian, "that if you do not please Oz, if he finds you foolish, if you waste his time, he will be very angry indeed, and when Oz is angry, he can be – how shall I put this? – most unpleasant, shall we say. With a click of his fingers, every single one of you could become nothing more than a puff of smoke. Poof! Poof! Poof! Poof! And Poof! The dog too. Five puffs of smoke. Think about that. You are well warned. But since you have asked to see him, I must take you to him. That is my duty." He opened a green chest beside him and took out a pair of green glasses. "Each of you must wear a pair of these, or else you will be blinded by the glare of our magnificent Emerald City. I have glasses of all sizes, for lions and dogs too." Then putting on a pair of glasses himself, he said with an imperious wave of his hand: "Follow me, and do not on any account remove your glasses." And so we entered the Emerald City.

"I just hope we're doing the right thing," whispered Scarecrow.

"So do I," said Dorothy.

As we walked down the street, I was looking into the shop windows. Green hats, green shoes, green dresses. Then I spotted something I liked: sausages, in a butcher's shop, green sausages. I'd have eaten any sausages by now – whatever their colour – I was so hungry. They looked so good, and I'd never had green sausages. I had to lick my lips to stop myself from dribbling. Lion, I noticed, was doing the same. That was all Lion and I were thinking of as we walked on into the Emerald City. We weren't thinking of the Great and Terrible Wizard of Oz.

We were thinking of sausages, lovely delicious green sausages.

I didn't like wearing those glasses at all, little puppies. I mean, dogs in glasses! We caught sight of ourselves in a shop window. Believe me, we looked stupid. But, all the same, it was a good thing we had those glasses on, little puppies, I can tell you. As I walked through the streets of the Emerald City, I had a peek over the top of them. I never saw anything so bright and shiny in all my life. The whole city glittered and sparkled in the sun. And of course everything was green, and I mean everything: green cobbles on the streets, green lamp-posts, green horses, green carts, and the people didn't just wear green clothes, they had green skin too. The lemonade on the street stalls was green, so were the children drinking it, and the popcorn and toffee apples and candyfloss green too, all of them.

The Guardian with the twirling green moustache led us on through the bustling streets, and everywhere we went, people pointed and stared at us as if we were

strangers from another world – which I suppose in a way we were, Dorothy and me anyway. They seemed quite afraid of us. Tin Woodman and Scarecrow waved at everyone cheerily, so no one seemed to be afraid of them. But I could see they were really terrified of Lion. I can't imagine why. He just looked funny in his glasses, not frightening at all, as he padded along beside me.

"Nice place, Toto," he said, "nice people too. But green's not my favourite colour. I'm hungry. I so want some of those green sausages."

"Me too," I told him with my eyes.

We came at last to the gates of the Palace of Oz, right in the centre of the city. The Guardian led us through the door of the palace and up a grand staircase into a huge hall where of course all the chairs and tables and carpets were green, the chandeliers too. "Wipe your feet," he told us. "The Great and Terrible Wizard of Oz does not like strangers anyway, but he particularly hates strangers with dirty feet."

So we wiped our feet and our paws very carefully so as not to upset the Great Wizard. We had to wait in this hall for some while, all sitting side by side on a green sofa, me on Dorothy's lap because I had kept wandering off around the room, just to snuffle about and explore, and the Guardian had said that the Great and Terrible Wizard of Oz did not like snuffling dogs, that snuffling dogs made him angry.

Everything the Guardian said about this great and terrible wizard did not sound good at all. By this time, all of us were getting really worried. He sounded so scary. I was trembling with fear. We all were, Lion most of all. I was so glad I was on Dorothy's lap, that she was stroking the top of my head and talking to me. "It'll be all right, Toto," she was whispering. "He can't be that terrible, he can't be." But she was humming now, so I could tell she was worried too.

Soon we were all humming, me as well in my own way, until the Guardian with the green and twirling moustache told us off. "Stop that dreadful noise at once. The Great and Terrible Wizard of Oz hates humming." So we sat there in silence, waiting and trembling, and Dorothy hugging me so tight I could hardly breathe. We seemed to be sitting there for ever, before we heard a gong sounding, echoing so loud through the palace that the walls and windows and the chandeliers seemed to shake with it.

"The Great and Terrible Wizard of Oz will see you now," said the Guardian. "Remember to bow low, very low," he added, "when you see the wizard and when you leave too."

"What will he look like?" Dorothy asked nervously.

"Whatever he wants to look like," replied the Guardian rather impatiently. "And another thing," he went on, "you speak only to answer his questions, and you do exactly as he says, understand? And don't gasp in astonishment at anything, and particularly do not say 'Wow'! He hates gasping and he hates 'Wow'. Argue and he will get angry. And if he gets angry, he will only have to click his fingers, like this – poof! – and you will go up in a puff of smoke, and that will be the end of you. Many strangers before you have gone in there and ended up as puffs of smoke." He led us to an arched doorway and opened the door. "In you go," he said. So in we went, slowly.

We found ourselves waiting in a vast room, green of course, with a high-vaulted ceiling, studded with brilliant emeralds so bright it hurt my eyes to look at them even through my glasses. At the far end of this great room, on a dais draped all around with green velvet, was a throne of green marble, and there was something or someone sitting on it, but we were too far away to see what or who it was.

"Bow," whispered Dorothy. "Bow very low." So they did. Not me though. Dogs don't bow to anyone, and anyway I couldn't because Dorothy was carrying me.

"Approach!" came a booming voice that echoed around the room. So we did, slowly. The something or someone on the throne turned out to be just about the weirdest thing I ever saw. It was a head, a massive bald head, that filled the throne. It had no arms, no legs, just a great head with a mouth and eyes and ears. It looked something like a giant egg, pearly-white and smooth, and not a hair to be seen. "Like a grumpy sort of Humpty Dumpty," Dorothy whispered. "I'm not afraid. I'm not afraid. I'm not afraid."

She kept saying this to herself as we walked slowly and trembling towards this strange and enormous head on the throne. The face frowned, the eyes glared, the mouth moved and spoke.

"I am the Wizard of Oz, Oz the Great, Oz the Terrible. Oz the All-powerful. Who are you? What have you come for? Speak!"

"I am Dorothy," Dorothy answered, her voice firm and full of courage – which surprised me and made me very proud. "And these are my good friends, Toto, Tin Woodman, Scarecrow and Lion."

The bald head leaned forward. "Those red shoes you are wearing," the mouth said. "Where did you get those from?"

So Dorothy told him our whole story, from the day the twister picked up our farmhouse in Kansas; the house falling accidentally on the Wicked Witch of the East in the land of the blue Munchkins, how the Good Witch of the North had kissed her and had given her the Wicked Witch's magic red shoes to protect her and us, how we had crossed deep black holes and rushing rivers, and had even escaped the cruel Kalidahs, how the Good Witch of the North in the land of the blue Munchkins had told us that the only way we could ever get home to Kansas was to go to the Emerald City and ask the Great and Terrible Wizard of Oz to help us, how Lion longed to have courage, how Tin Woodman so wanted a heart and how Scarecrow yearned to have some brains. She told it all very fast and it was a bit jumbled.

"Could you help us, please, sir?" Dorothy asked, rather breathlessly when she had finished. "I so want to go home and so does Toto."

"And I so want to have courage," said Lion.

"And I so want to have a heart," said Tin Woodman.

"And I really want some brains," said Scarecrow.

"Please, sir, we'd be ever so grateful," said Dorothy.

"Turn round," the head commanded us, blinking slowly three times, "while I think about this. I don't like strangers looking at me while I'm thinking, and mind you don't turn back till I tell you."

So we all did as we were told and turned round. We stood there, wondering, waiting. Then, after a while, came another voice from behind us, a woman's voice this time.

"Very well, you may turn and gaze upon me now."
And when we turned round the giant head was gone
and in its place on the throne sat the loveliest and most
radiant of ladies, in a long green gown of finest silk,
with shining green hair and on her head, a crown of
glorious emeralds. We all gasped.

"Wow!" we said all together.

Although I'm thinking mine sounded more
like "woof".

The lovely lady frowned at us. "Do you all want to
be pooffed into puffs of smoke?" she said, lifting
her hand, her fingers ready to click.

We all shook our heads. "Please no!" cried Dorothy.
"We didn't mean it, honest."

"I can see you are honest," the lovely lady said.
"But don't do it again. No more 'wows', understand?
Now tell me why I, the Great and Terrible Wizard of Oz,
should help you, who are nothing but strangers to me?"

"Because," Dorothy explained, and I could tell she was thinking hard, "because you are good, and kind and wise and powerful, and because we need your help. Back in Kansas, Aunt Em always told me to be good and kind, and always to help anyone who asks for it, particularly if they need help very badly, and we do."

"Turn round again then," said the lovely lady, "while I think about it. I don't like anyone looking at me while I'm thinking."

So we turned round again, and waited, and waited, none of us daring to look before we were told to. "I have thought about it," came a voice, after a while, but not a woman's voice this time, in fact hardly a voice at all, more a raging roar. "Turn round now!" So we did, in fear and trembling, and saw sitting on the throne a most dreadful-looking beast, as big as an elephant, with the head and horn of a rhinoceros, with green woolly hair covering its whole body, with five eyes in its head, five arms and five legs. We almost gasped but stopped ourselves just in time. We almost said "wow" too, but managed not to, only just.

"I have thought about this," growled this terrible beast, "and I have decided I will help you, but only if you help me."

"How can we possibly help you?" Dorothy asked. "You are the Great and Terrible Wizard of Oz.

Surely you can do anything you wish? You can even change what you look like, click your fingers and make puffs of smoke of us. How can we possibly help you?"

"No one asks the Great and Terrible Wizard of Oz a question," roared the beast. "Have you no manners? I ask the questions, I say what is to happen. Understand? Or do you wish to be puffs of smoke?"

"No, please," Dorothy begged. "Don't be angry. We will do whatever you want us to do, or try to anyway."

"Very well, that is better," growled the beast, but his growl was slightly gentler now. "You have already got rid of the Wicked Witch of the East, which was good. Now you will find and do the same with the Wicked Witch of the West. Get rid of her. You have the power – even my great powers cannot overcome her spells. Yours can. You told me you have been kissed by the Good Witch of the North. And I see the mark of it still on your forehead, so you cannot be harmed.

And you have those magic red shoes. Wear them and you will have all the power you need to dispose of the Wicked Witch of the West. Do this for me, and bring me proof you have done it, and I will help you get home to Kansas, you and your dog. Tin Woodman can have his heart, and you, Scarecrow, can have your brains, and you, Lion, you can have the courage of the king of the beasts. All this I promise you. Now, turn and go. And don't look back!"

We turned and walked the length of that room together, and all the time I was thinking: *Don't look back, Toto, don't look back.* But I'm never very good at doing what I'm told, especially when I don't want to do it, so just as we reached the door, I had a crafty, sneaky look behind me. The head on the throne, the lovely lady, the horrible beast, had become a great ball of flaming fire. "Toto!" came a thundering voice filling the room, filling the whole palace as we walked out.

Uh-oh, I thought. *Now I'm in trouble, big trouble.*

"Toto, you looked back!" roared the Wizard of Oz. You are a naughty dog, a very naughty dog, and I should be very angry with you. And I am. But although I am the Great and Terrible Wizard of Oz, I can be kind and merciful when I like to be. So for Dorothy's sake, for she is a kind and honest girl who loves you like a best friend, I will not make a puff of smoke of you – this time!"

Well, as you can imagine, I did not look round again. I was mighty pleased after that to get out of the Palace of Oz alive, and soon we were on our way back to the city gates through the streets of the Emerald City. At the gates, still trembling after all that had happened, we handed our glasses back to the Guardian with the twirling green moustache. "Where are you off to now?" he asked us as he opened the gates to let us out.

"West, I suppose," said Dorothy, "because somehow we have to find and get rid of the Wicked Witch of the West. We don't want to, but we have to, or the

Wizard of Oz won't help us."

The Guardian laughed at that, laughed loud and long, laughed fit to bust. "You, do away with the Wicked Witch of the West? What, a tin man, a scarecrow, a slip of a girl, a trembly lion and a little bitty dog?" I nearly bit him then just to show him, but Dorothy told me not to.

"Pay him no attention," she whispered to me. "He's a rude, rude man."

"We won't be seeing you again then, will we!" the Guardian sneered, twiddling his twirling green moustache. "That Wicked Witch of the West will have you lot for breakfast. She'll see you coming a mile away through her all-seeing eye. She sees everyone coming, and once she's seen you, you don't stand a chance. She'll send her horrible creatures after you."

"We'll show her," said Dorothy, linking arms with Tin Woodman and Scarecrow. "Won't we?"

"Yes, Dorothy," they said.

"Yes," I told her with my eyes. But we only agreed

with her to make her feel better, to make us all feel better. They all felt as I felt, I could tell. We none of us believed we could do it, none of us. But all of us knew we had to try.

"Which road do we take?" Dorothy asked the Guardian with the twirling green moustache. "How do we find this witch?"

"There is no road," replied the Guardian. "Just go west towards the setting sun, and, believe me, she will find you with her all-seeing eye. As soon as you are in her country, the country of the yellow Winkies, she will know

you are there, and she will either destroy you or make slaves of you, whichever she feels like doing. She magics her horrible creatures out of dust, out of thin air – you won't stand a chance against them."

"Oh, stop trying to frighten us," said Dorothy, stamping her foot at him crossly. "It's not fair and it's not kind. We are going. I have the kiss of the Good Witch of the North on my forehead and the red shoes of the Wicked Witch of the East on my feet. Nothing the Wicked Witch of the West can do can harm us. That's what the Great and Terrible Wizard of Oz told us. Oh yes," she went on, "and by the way your moustache is far too long and twirling, that's what I think. You should cut it. You'll be a much nicer person altogether with a shorter moustache, not so proud and hoity-toity, not so unkind!"

"Do you really think so?" said the Guardian, fingering his moustache rather nervously now. He seemed very upset and taken aback. "Maybe I shall then, if you say so. Pardon my rudeness, please. I did not mean to be unkind. I must say, you are the bravest people I've ever met, for the Wicked Witch of the West is the wickedest witch there ever was. I wish you well. I wish you all the luck in the world. You will need it." And off he went.

"Well," said Dorothy, clapping her hands to cheer us all up. "Up we get and off we go!"

And so off we went, westwards towards the country of the yellow Winkies, towards the country of the Wicked Witch of the West, where her horrible creatures would be waiting for us. It was hard to be cheerful. But Dorothy wanted us to be, so we were, or so we pretended to be.

CHAPTER ELEVEN

The Wickedest Witch
There Ever Was

*N*ow this bit does get quite alarming, little
puppies. So, if you don't want to hear it,
now's the time to put your paws over your
ears. That's what Lion used to do whenever
things became too frightening for him.

We had no road to follow, only
the sun. The grass was soft to
walk on, and there were
daisies and buttercups

everywhere. The birds were twittering and cooing, the larks trilling as they rose into the blue above us, and along the sparkling streams the dippers were dipping and kingfishers flashing by. It was the most beautiful countryside we had walked through in all our long journey.

It was hard to believe anything bad could happen to us in this country. Our spirits rose, our steps quickened. By now we had left the Emerald City far behind us, and were up in the hills, where suddenly the way was full of stones, and rockier altogether, which made for harder, rougher walking. Tin Woodman often stumbled to his knees and had to be helped up. Dorothy took his arm, but then she would stumble, and he would have to help her up. Higher and higher we climbed, the sun beating down on us, every hill steeper than the one before, and now the wind was howling about us. Soon we were all tired out. We found a more sheltered place out of the wind, in amongst the rocks, where a carpet of soft thrift had grown. We lay down to sleep, all of us huddling together.

Even Scarecrow lay down with us, which was unusual. "I don't like wind," he said. "I'm so light I could get blown away."

We had just settled down to sleep when I thought I heard a whistling sound. I imagined at first it must be the whistling of the wind around the rocks. Then I was sure I was hearing the howling of wolves. *No, I thought, that's just the wind again. Don't worry about it,* I told myself. I curled up closer to Dorothy and fell fast asleep, which was when I dreamed a horrible dream. I dreamed I saw the Wicked Witch of the West, a warty old witch in a pointed hat and pointed shoes with one huge eye in the middle of her forehead. She was blowing on a silver whistle, and all around her the air thickened and swirled into clouds, grey clouds, that turned into howling wolves.

"I see strangers in my land," she was shrieking, "strangers lying asleep on my thrift in amongst my rocks. They are no good to me as slaves for one is made of tin, another of straw, one is a raggedy old lion, and the other a little bitty dog, and a slip of a girl, none of them any use to anyone. Go, my dears," she screeched, "go and tear them to pieces."

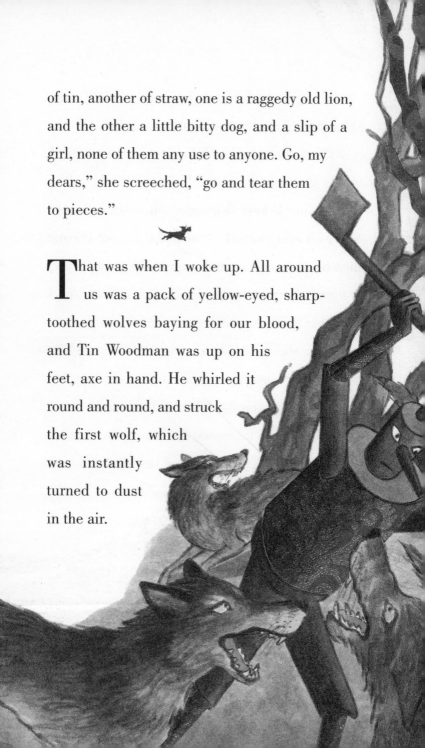

That was when I woke up. All around us was a pack of yellow-eyed, sharp-toothed wolves baying for our blood, and Tin Woodman was up on his feet, axe in hand. He whirled it round and round, and struck the first wolf, which was instantly turned to dust in the air.

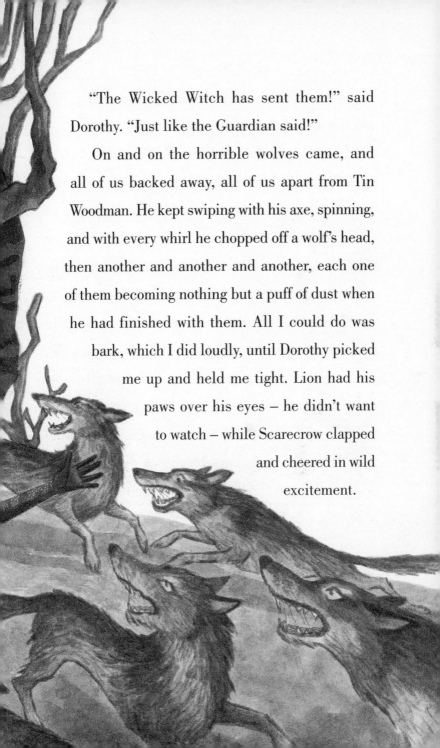

"The Wicked Witch has sent them!" said Dorothy. "Just like the Guardian said!"

On and on the horrible wolves came, and all of us backed away, all of us apart from Tin Woodman. He kept swiping with his axe, spinning, and with every whirl he chopped off a wolf's head, then another and another and another, each one of them becoming nothing but a puff of dust when he had finished with them. All I could do was bark, which I did loudly, until Dorothy picked me up and held me tight. Lion had his paws over his eyes – he didn't want to watch – while Scarecrow clapped and cheered in wild excitement.

"Bravo, Tin Woodman! Bravo!" he was shouting.

"I'm awfully scared," said Lion.

And Dorothy was sobbing, her face buried in my neck. "Horrible! Horrible!" she cried. "The Wicked Witch of the West can make wolves out of dust."

Tin Woodman sat down, exhausted. "Good axe this," he said. "Came in handy, didn't it? Sorry if I upset you, Dorothy. But it was either the wolves or us."

"This means she knows we are here," said Dorothy, looking around her. "The Guardian was right. She can see us with her all-seeing eye. She's seeing us now." And this was true, of course. I knew that much from my dream.

All the next day we walked up hill and down dale, fording rivers and streams. So by sundown we were exhausted all over again, and I was hungry too, as I tried often to remind Dorothy with my pleading eyes, with my cold, cold nose. But she was too tired to care about anything, even me. Again we all lay down to sleep, arms around one another, me with my head on Dorothy's lap. I was asleep at once. I thought I heard a whistle blowing, and then the sound of crows cawing.

And then I dreamed a horrible dream again, but not the same dream. This time that warty old Wicked Witch of the West was up on the yellow ramparts of her yellow castle, and looking out towards us with her one huge telescopic eye. And I could see what she was seeing. All her wolf guards were reduced to dust now, and all of us were lying there fast asleep, me too, my head on Dorothy's lap! I could see myself in my own dream!

Shaking with rage, she blew again on her silver whistle. "Those infernal strangers! They have defeated my wolves!" She pointed to the skies and shrieked a spell. Above her, crows gathered out of the darkening clouds.

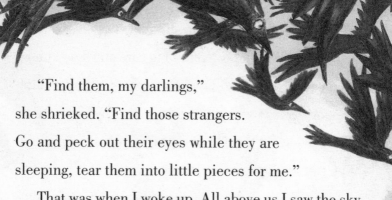

"Find them, my darlings,"
she shrieked. "Find those strangers.
Go and peck out their eyes while they are
sleeping, tear them into little pieces for me."

That was when I woke up. All above us I saw the sky
filled with crows, dozens of them, all with black beady
eyes and cruel beaks, and they were cawing at us, diving
on us. Scarecrow was up on his feet, arms outstretched.
"Don't you worry, my friends," he cried. "It's what I'm
for, remember? I scare crows, don't I? I won't let them
hurt you." And for a while it seemed to be working.

The crows flew around and around us, cawing
angrily, and they didn't dare attack.

But then the biggest of them, the king crow, cawed
out. "He's not a real man at all! Look at him! He's just
a straw man! He can't harm us!" And he flew down
and started stabbing and pecking at Scarecrow, pulling
out his straw. That made Scarecrow really mad, really

cross. He reached up and took king crow by the neck, and shook him, until king crow cawed no more and was nothing but a puff of dust. That only angered the other crows even more, and they all came down to try to peck Scarecrow to pieces, and Scarecrow did the same to all of them. By the time he had finished, there were no crows left, not even a feather, just a lot of dust lying around.

"I'm awfully scared," said Lion. "I've never liked crows."

"Bravo, Scarecrow! Bravo!" cried Tin Woodman.

"That's that then," said Scarecrow.

"The Wicked Witch of the West sent them," said Dorothy. "I know she did." And again I knew from my dream she was right.

All next day we walked, wondering all the while what nasty wicked plans the Wicked Witch had in mind for us, and trying not to worry about it, which was impossible, of course. Dorothy was worried too, though she never said it. She just hummed a lot – a sure sign she was worried. She sang a bit too, to keep us all cheerful, I think.

Her singing never made me cheerful, if I'm honest. But the others seemed to like it. Lion and I found a rabbit or two to chase – and eat out of sight of the others – and that kept me a lot more cheerful. Dorothy seemed quite happy with the apples and pears she found, and Tin Woodman and Scarecrow didn't bother with food, so they were fine. We none of us looked forward to the sunset though. Whatever the Wicked Witch had in store for us was going to happen after sunset, we knew that. And sunset comes, whether you want it to or not.

"Home is home, isn't it, Toto?" said Dorothy, sadly. "And home is best. Home is where I want to be, want to be so much."

Me too, me too, I was thinking. I gave her a lick on her hand to let her know. She patted my head. At least I had Dorothy, at least we had each other.

We cuddled tight together, but, tired though we all were, I think I was the only one who fell asleep, and when I did, I dreamed a horrible dream once more. The Wicked Witch of the West was up on the yellow ramparts of her yellow castle again, her all-seeing eye spotting us at once, all of us asleep. She blew loud and long and shrilly on her silver whistle, pointed to the sky and screamed a spell. At once a great cloud of bees gathered about her, humming and roaring so loud it might have been thunder, swarming around the castle ramparts. "The strangers have destroyed my crows," she screeched. "Go, bees," she commanded. "Go at once, and sting them to death, that little bitty dog too, all of them."

That was the moment I woke up, and there above us was a huge swarm of black bees. *Now we were done for*, I thought, *now there was no escape*. Nothing could save us.

But Scarecrow and Tin Woodman were up on their feet, and Scarecrow was pulling out handfuls of straw

from inside himself and shouting at Dorothy and me
and Lion.

"Lie where you are, be still, and Tin Woodman and
I will cover you completely with straw. None of the
bees will sting you." So we did as Scarecrow told us, as
he and Tin Woodman covered us all over with a thick
blanket of straw, so when the bees flew down to attack,
we were all safely hidden away and protected. There

was only Tin Woodman left to sting – and a rather thin and bedraggled Scarecrow – and bees, of course, can't sting straw any more than they can sting tin. In their fury they tried to sting Tin Woodman, though, and every time they tried, their stings broke against the tin, and of course everyone knows that once a bee has used his sting he dies. But these bees didn't die like real bees do, they just turned to dust, like the wolves had, like the crows had.

"Bravo!" Dorothy cried, and Lion roared, and I woofed, woofed like crazy I was so happy, so relieved. I really do not like bees – never have.

We soon stuffed all the straw back into Scarecrow, so that he looked much as he had before, even better I thought.

Bees, crows, wolves, whatever the Wicked Witch of the West sent out to attack us, we had defeated. It must have been Dorothy's magic red shoes, or that kiss from the Good Witch of the North, that had protected us, but I thought it was also because we looked after one another, that together we were strong, too strong for the Wicked Witch of the West.

She tried once more the next evening to destroy us, sending forty of her slaves, the yellow Winkies, to attack us with their bows and arrows, with their pointed spears and sharp swords. But Lion simply stood there and roared at them, and they dropped all their bows and arrows and spears and swords and ran away. When they had all gone we were so happy. We danced round and round, and sang and whooped and clanked and barked and roared, until we were quite giddy – and I chased my tail, which made me giddy too. We were all of us giddy with joy. We were all sure by now – surely we were sure – that the Wicked Witch of the West had done her best time and time again to get rid of us and had failed.

How wrong we were.

CHAPTER TWELVE

We Fall into the Clutches of the Wicked Witch of the West

I'm afraid things often get worse, my dear little *puppies, before they get better. It's like that, in real life as well as in stories. And of course this story is real life as well as a story.* We thought the worst was over, that things could only get better now. And that's how it looked. We walked on day after day, always going westwards towards the setting sun, finding enough to eat and drink on the way. We had tired feet, or paws, but that didn't matter.

We were happy enough as we marched along. After all, we thought, we had overcome the worst the Wicked Witch of the West could do to us.

And then one night I had another horrible dream. I saw in my dream the warty Wicked Witch in her castle hall shouting and screaming at her yellow Winkie slaves. She was standing before them, hands on hips, a golden cap on her head.

"You have failed me, you miserable slaves," she shrieked. "But now I have my magic golden cap on, which never fails me. Whoever owns this cap – and I own it – can command the terrible Winged Monkeys, but just three times. Once I commanded them and they gave me you, my yellow Winkies, my army of slaves, so that you could build me my yellow castle, so that I could rule over this country and make it mine. Then I commanded them to drive the Great and Terrible Wizard of Oz far away, to the Emerald City, so that his power could never harm me. And that they did. Now I shall speak the spell and they will do my bidding for the third and last time."

She stood on her left foot and wiggled her right. "Eppepeppekakki!" she cackled loudly. "Hillohollohello! Zizzyzuzzyzik!" The sky darkened, then lightning flashed, thunder roared, hailstones rained down. She looked up and pointed. "See, my Winkie slaves, they come!" she screeched. And out of the storm came a great rushing of wings. I thought at first in my dream that the sky above her must be full of ravens, cawing and chattering. Then all of a sudden the sun shone through, and all around the Wicked Witch I could see they were not ravens at all, but monkeys, flying monkeys! They sat around her now in the vaulted hall of her castle, a crowd of monkeys, huge monkeys with angry eyes and bared teeth.

"You called?" The voice I heard seemed to come from everywhere, from all of them, at the same time. "Remember, this is your last time, Witch. What do you wish us to do?"

"Go, Winged Monkeys, go to the strangers you will

find sleeping out there in my country," shrieked the Wicked Witch of the West. "I command you to kill them for me, all except for the lion. He may be useful. At least he is strong. He can be my slave. He can be harnessed like a horse and pull a cart. The rest are useless to me. Destroy them! Destroy!"

And at once the Winged Monkeys flapped their great wings, lifted off and flew out of the windows of the great hall, out over the ramparts and over the hills beyond, until they saw us lying there, curled up together on the ground, fast asleep. They were coming for us!

I woke then, woken by the fear of them in my dream, by the wind of wings and the chattering and hissing of monkeys. I wasn't sure whether I was still inside my dream or not. But Dorothy was screaming and clutching me to her. It wasn't a dream! Lion was roaring his anger and defiance, and the giant Winged

Monkeys had already caught Scarecrow and were pulling the straw out of him, out of his clothes, out of his head. They made a bundle of his blue clothes and tossed them up into the top of a tree. Then they picked up Tin Woodman, flew him to a great height and dropped him down on to the rocks below where he shattered into pieces, nothing but a pile of twisted, dented bits of tin. They dropped a net over Lion and caught him, and then, lifting him up into the air, they flew him away over the hills.

"Oh, Toto," cried Dorothy, her eyes full of tears. "Look what they have done. We have lost Scarecrow and Tin Woodman and Lion, and they were such good, kind friends."

I wanted to comfort her, but I was as sad as she was. Besides there was no time. The Winged Monkeys were coming for us now, landing all around us, and closing in, closer, closer, chattering and hissing menacingly. Well, I wasn't having that, was I? They were attacking Dorothy!

I went for them, snarling and snapping at their feet, at their wings, but they just ignored me, and reached out their big hairy arms to grab Dorothy. I thought they were going to tear her to pieces. Suddenly, though, the chattering stopped, the hissing too, and they backed away, bowing their heads.

"We can't touch her," said the tallest and hairiest of the Winged Monkeys. "Look, see her red shoes, and see on her forehead the mark where the Good Witch of the North has kissed her. This child cannot be harmed." He looked down at me – I was still snapping at him. "Is this creature a friend of yours?"

Dorothy nodded. "My best friend," she said, trying to hold back her tears. "My only friend in the world. You have killed the others."

"Then we shall not harm him." And before we knew it, the Winged Monkeys had picked us both up, and, gently cradling us in their arms, were flying us up through the clouds and over the hills towards a yellow castle in the distance. It all happened so fast, I had

no time to be frightened. Soon we were landing on the ramparts of this great yellow castle, the one I had seen.

"Lion!" cried Dorothy. "Thank goodness! At least Lion survived."

The Winged Monkeys set us down, Dorothy and me, on our feet right in front of the Wicked Witch of the West.

"We have done as you commanded us," said the leader of the Winged Monkeys. "The tin woodman and the scarecrow we both destroyed." Hearing it said like that made us sadder still, Dorothy and me. But it made us angrier too. "And the lion, as you see, is now your slave to do with as you please. But this girl has the kiss of the Good Witch on her forehead, and she wears the red shoes. So we cannot harm her, even if we wanted to, which we don't. And the little bitty dog there is her best friend, so he is also protected. You have now used up your three commandments, Witch, so we will do no more for you. And we are glad of it. No witch was ever wickeder than you." And without another word, all the Winged Monkeys rose into the clouds above and were gone.

The Wicked Witch came up close to Dorothy, to look her in the face. She saw too the mark of the Good Witch's kiss on her forehead, and she saw the red shoes on her feet. I could see she was frightened, and that she was pretending not to be. Dorothy couldn't see it, but I could. Dogs have a sixth sense, don't we? I could see the Wicked Witch was already concocting some cunning plan.

"I could kill you and I could kill your little dog too," the witch told Dorothy, "but I have decided, in the kindness of my heart, that I won't. Instead you will slave for me in the kitchen, do the washing-up, scrub the floors. You will polish, fetch water, keep the fire going. You will do as I wish or you and your little bitty dog will end up like that tin man and that scarecrow out there on the hillside, all in little bitty bits and pieces."

Dorothy didn't cry in front of the witch. She put a brave face on it. But, over the days that followed, she cried quietly to herself as she slaved away for the Wicked Witch of the West, crying herself to sleep every night. "Oh, Toto, how I wish I was back home with Aunt Em and Uncle Henry," she'd often tell me. "Poor Lion is in his cage, and poor Scarecrow, poor Tin Woodman, when I think what has happened to them, I am so unhappy, Toto. But I shall work ever so hard, then the Wicked Witch will not harm you. To lose you as well would break my heart in two."

I touched my nose against her cheek so she knew I felt the same about her.

We were well guarded all the time by those yellow Winkies, the Wicked Witch's slaves. They weren't nasty to us exactly, but they weren't that kind to us either. They were always gruff with us, and always so sad and miserable. And being yellow I suppose, they smelt of custard too, which I didn't much like, still don't.

The Wicked Witch smelt strongly of vinegar, which suited her, because vinegar is the worst smell in all the world. If ever I barked at her, which I did because I hated her, the Wicked Witch would beat me with her umbrella.

I managed to bite her more than once, but she did not bleed. All her blood had dried up long ago. She bled red dust. Not nice.

She was so cruel. Time and again, she would poke Lion through the bars of his cage with her umbrella, because he refused to be harnessed like a horse and would roar at her and tell her just what he thought of her. She starved him then, just to punish him. At night, when the Wicked Witch and all the Winkies were asleep, Dorothy and I would creep down into the courtyard to comfort him and to bring him food from the kitchen.

"We will get you out somehow, Lion," Dorothy told him. "I'll find a way."

And I knew she would too, somehow. But how, that was the question. I never saw Dorothy as unhappy as she was then. I did all I could to make her feel better. I never left her side all day, snuggled up close to her at night, touched her cheek with my cold, cold nose, licked her ear. I didn't really care where I was, in the Wicked Witch's castle, in the Land of Oz or back in Kansas, I just wanted her to be happy. And I knew she never would be, and neither would I be, until we were home again.

Dogs have a sixth sense, one more than people do. I sensed, before Dorothy ever did, what the Wicked Witch of the West was up to. I could see her

eyeing Dorothy's red shoes, and I guessed why. Dorothy loved those shoes so much she never took them off, even in bed. Sometimes at night, when I was half awake, I would see the Wicked Witch stealing into our room, and would growl at her, baring my teeth. She did not like my teeth, not one bit. But I couldn't stay awake all the time. I tried to, but I couldn't. And early one morning when Dorothy and I were still both fast asleep, she crept in, and before I could wake up and bite her, she had reached down and snatched one of the red shoes.

"Aha!" she shrieked, waving the shoe triumphantly in the air. "Now you have only half your power. I have the rest." And she danced around the room cackling at us.

Well, that was too much for me. I went after her. I bit her hand and her leg, her ankle, and that made her hopping mad. The Wicked Witch lashed out at me then with her umbrella, again and again, and that made Dorothy really angry. She leapt out of the bed, shouting at her.

"First you kill Tin Woodman and Scarecrow, and imprison our friend Lion. Then you make a slave of me, then you steal one of my red shoes, and now you beat Toto. I have had enough."

"Not a great idea," Scarecrow had told her, "just a simple one. I haven't any brains, but I do have simple ideas from time to time."

She was as angry as I've ever seen her. She was looking around for something, anything she could use to fight off the Wicked Witch. Then I had an idea, which turned out to be a brilliant idea, just about the best one I ever had. There was a bucket in the corner full of rainwater that leaked from the roof – I'd had a drink from it earlier. I ran towards it, nudged it with my nose, woofed and woofed till Dorothy looked. She knew what to do now. She grabbed the bucket and

threw freezing-cold water all over the witch.

The witch was soaked through, dripping wet from her pointed hat to her pointed toes. She was capering all about the room, trying to brush the water off herself, and she was shaking the red slipper at us, cursing at us loudly, screeching and shrieking. Then the strangest thing happened. The shrieking and the screeching became a wailing and a whimpering, and in front of our eyes this cruel Wicked Witch began to sob like a child. And then she began to shrink.

"Oh no," she cried pitifully, sinking to the ground. "Water may be life for everyone else. But water is death to me. It is melting me away! It is the end of me, the end of all my power, all my wickedness." Soon all that was left of her was the red shoe lying on the floor in a puddle of water, and a fading smell of vinegar.

Dorothy picked up the red shoe and slipped it on.

"Aunt Em said I should never lose my temper," she said,

"but do you know, Toto, I'm very glad I did. Let's go. Let's rescue Lion from his cage and then let's get out of here, back to the Wizard of Oz. Then home, Toto, home. Home is home, and home is best, right, Toto?"

It was so good to hear her say that again. "You're so dog-gone right," I woofed. I woofed it and woofed it.

CHAPTER THIRTEEN

Promises, Promises

*B*ut it wasn't as simple as all that, little *puppies, because these yellow Winkies, being the Wicked Witch's slaves, would not let us go that easily.* We ran down to the courtyard to rescue Lion from his cage, and there we found hundreds of yellow Winkies, with their spears and their bows and arrows, and not looking at all friendly. "What have you done with the Wicked Witch of the West?" the chief of the Winkies demanded.

"We have put an end to her, washed her away, you might say," Dorothy told them. "And it was all thanks to Toto here."

I do love you, Dorothy, I was thinking.

She turned to the Winkies. "You are slaves no more, Winkies."

At this they gave us a great cheer, and after they had opened the cage and let Lion out, they insisted we stay for a party, to thank us and to celebrate their new-found freedom. But I could tell during the festivities that Dorothy was far from happy, despite all the dancing and singing and laughter that was going on all around us. I wasn't the only one who had noticed it.

"Why are you so sad, Dorothy?" the chief Winkie asked.

"I am thinking of poor Scarecrow and poor Tin Woodman," she replied sadly. "They should be here celebrating with us. I can't sing and dance knowing they are out there somewhere alone in the hills, our dear Tin Woodman all battered and broken, and our dear Scarecrow all pulled apart and all unstuffed and not himself at all."

"You and your friends have done so much for us, Dorothy," said the chief Winkie. "So now we will help you. We will find Tin Woodman, and Scarecrow, and put them together again, you'll see."

And do you know, little puppies, those wonderful yellow Winkies did just that. They went out looking at once, and the very next day, a search party of yellow Winkies discovered Tin Woodman – or what was left of him – lying all in bits, broken and battered and dented in amongst the rocks. They gathered him up, and carried every last piece of him back to the castle.

Three Winkie tin-smiths soon knocked out the dents, put him together again, fixed him up and oiled his joints and his axe, because, after all this time out in the wind and the rain, Tin Woodman had rusted up pretty bad. But even when they had finished, he still looked a bit battered and not quite himself, and he couldn't move at all.

"He's still not himself," cried Dorothy. "What can we do?"

The Winkies all shook their heads. "We do not know," said one of them. "But perhaps if you do a little tap dance in your magic red shoes, and wish very hard . . . then maybe, maybe . . . Just an idea."

And so Dorothy did just that and at once Tin Woodman opened his eyes!

"I feel awfully stiff," he said, "but I think I'm fine." He waggled his arms, his legs, his head. "I'm fine! I'm fine!"

Did I woof! Did Dorothy hug him! Did all the yellow Winkies clap and cheer!

Then the yellow Winkies, who by now had come to like Tin Woodman very much, decided they would paint him yellow, bright yellow as they all were, so he would feel like one of them.

Tin Woodman loved his new look. "I look like the sun," he said, preening himself. "Thank you, Winkies, thank you so very much."

And meanwhile, another search party of yellow
Winkies soon found Scarecrow's bundle of clothes up
in a tall tree. They gathered some good clean fresh
straw and stuffed him again so that Scarecrow was
soon full of himself once more, if you understand my
meaning. Again, he didn't come to life straight away,
but when Dorothy did another tap dance in her red
shoes, and wished hard, he was soon blinking in the
light and marvelling at being there, in the castle,
though he said he had far too little brains to work
out why he was here, he was just glad that everyone

was back together again and the Wicked Witch was gone.

I couldn't believe how kind these yellow Winkies turned out to be. When they were the Witch's slaves, they had been sullen and sad and not at all friendly, but now they were all smiles, and fun and laughter. "Just shows you," said Dorothy, "how powerful a thing is a little bit of freedom."

"I know how they feel, Dorothy," Lion agreed. "When you are behind bars, when you are not free, you have nothing to live for. To be free is everything. It makes them happy, look at them. And it makes me happy too – almost as happy as food!"

I woofed in agreement. The only thing missing for me was sausages.

They wanted us to stay, the yellow Winkies, but Dorothy told them we had to go, to get back as soon as we could to the Great and Terrible Wizard of Oz. "I so long to go back home to Kansas," she explained. "And Scarecrow longs for some brains, and Tin Woodman longs for a heart, and Lion so wants some courage. You see, the Wizard of Oz promised us all these things if we killed the Wicked Witch of the West. Well, now we have."

And those kind-hearted Winkies fed us like kings before we left, and gave us food for the journey. They gave each of us gifts too – Tin Woodman, a special silver oil can full of oil because they thought it would come in handy in an emergency and, the Winkies told him, that now that he was yellow, he should come back to see them whenever he felt like it. To Scarecrow, they gave garlands of beautiful flowers; to Lion, some throat medicine because they thought his throat must get sore with all his roaring.

And as for me, I got a yellow bouncing ball that Dorothy could throw for me to chase. To Dorothy they gave the Wicked Witch's magic golden cap, so that if she ever needed the Winged Monkeys, she could

call on them for help three times. Dorothy thanked the yellow Winkies for all of us, and put on her new golden cap instead of her bonnet – it suited her much better, I thought; I never much liked her in that bonnet – and off we went out through the gates of the yellow castle, their cheering and well-wishing ringing in our ears.

But finding our way back to the Emerald City was a problem. We did not know the country at all. After all, if you remember, those Winged Monkeys had picked us up and flown us over hill and dale, stream and forest, to the Wicked Witch's yellow castle in the West. There was no yellow brick road to follow, and there was not even a path through the meadows.

"East," said Scarecrow, scratching his head. "We were going west to get here, right? So to get back we must go east. But the sun is right over our heads, isn't it? So we still can't tell east from west. Which way do we go?"

"Follow me," said Lion. So we did, but we soon found ourselves right back where we started. We'd just gone round in a circle.

"Follow me," said Tin Woodman. "I know the way." But he didn't.

"Follow me," said Dorothy, but we got lost again.

After a while wandering around getting lost in this unknown country, we all sat down in deep despair.

"Now we'll never get back to the Wizard of Oz, and I'll never get home," Dorothy said sadly.

"And I shall be brainless for ever," sighed Scarecrow.

"And I shall be heartless for ever," Tin Woodman cried.

"And I shall be a coward for ever," Lion said, whimpering miserably. We were all tired, and sad as well. I was too tired even to chase rabbits and butterflies. But a squeaking little mouse that came skittering right past me was too much of a temptation. I was up and after it in a flash.

"That gives me an idea," said Scarecrow, scratching his head again. "Didn't the Queen of the field mice, who helped us once, say that if ever we needed her again we should call for her? We are lost, aren't we? We need her help. Let's ask her."

"Brilliant, Scarecrow!" cried Dorothy. "We'll all call for her." So we did, each in our own way. I barked, the lion roared. There was a long silence once the echoes had died away, and then we heard a squeaking and a rustling in the grass, and suddenly the little field mice were there, all around us, all over our feet and paws, and there was the Queen of the field mice herself, sitting at Dorothy's feet and looking up at her.

"You called?" she squeaked. Dorothy crouched down and explained everything to her, how we were lost, how the Wicked Witch of the West was dead, and how we had to get back as quick as possible to the Emerald City, to see the Great Wizard.

"Why are you asking me?" said the Queen of the field mice. "You have the answer on your head, girl, that golden cap. That is the magic golden cap of the Wicked Witch of the West, isn't it? It's easy. You just say the magic words to make the Winged Monkeys come, and then command them to take you there, to the Emerald City. Simple."

"What magic words?" Dorothy asked.

The Queen of the field mice thought for a bit. "I think I remember. Try: 'Eppepeppekakki. Hillohollohello. Zizzyzuzzyzik.' You're the owner of the golden cap. You're wearing it. The spell will work only for you. You have to get the words just right, mind." So Dorothy tried. She tried once, twice. We all looked up in the sky for the Winged Monkeys, and waited. There was no sign of them, no flapping of great wings, no chattering as they came.

It was no good. It seemed that nothing would ever get us home to Aunt Em and Uncle Henry.

"I don't like to correct you," said the Queen of the field mice, "but I think you said 'Zizzyzuzzyzuk'. It shouldn't be 'zuk' at the end, but 'zik'. It should be 'Zizzyzuzzyzik'. And I think for the spell to work you have to stand on your left foot only, and wiggle your right. Try again."

So Dorothy closed her eyes tight shut, concentrated very hard and stood on one leg, and said the magic spell again.

At once they came. Down through the clouds flew the Winged Monkeys, chattering. I didn't like them one bit, I never had, with their hairy arms,

their great flapping wings,
and their pointed ears – like
huge, ugly chattering bats they
were. I barked at them ferociously,
and couldn't wait to have a go at
them, give one of them a good bite when they
landed. Dorothy picked me up and held me tight as
they came down all around us.

"You called?" said the leader. "What is your
command?"

"To take us to the Emerald City as fast as you can,"
Dorothy told him, clutching me tightly because she
knew very well it was biting I had in mind.

Before we knew it, those Winged Monkeys had
picked us up and we were being flown away, the little
field mice below waving goodbye to us and becoming
littler with every moment. I've never been so frightened
in all my life. Up through the clouds we were flown,
higher and higher. I closed my eyes, and just hoped my

Winged Monkey would not drop me. I'd seen what they had once done to Tin Woodman, remember?

Then, after a while, I forgot I was frightened, and the gentle rhythmic swish of their wings sent me to sleep. When I woke, I was being set down on my feet outside the great green gates of the Emerald City, and we were all standing there, looking in amazement at one another, the Winged Monkeys flying off up into the clouds above us.

"Well," said Tin Woodman, shaking himself, trying out all his joints to make sure they were all still working. "How was your flight, my friends?"

"First class," said Dorothy, patting her golden cap and looking up at the great green gates of the Emerald City. "Useful, this golden cap, isn't it? And I can still call on those Winged Monkeys twice more, if we need them. Just so long as I don't forget the spell. Isn't it wonderful? They brought us all the way back. Now, let's not waste any time. Let's go right in to see the Great and Terrible Wizard of Oz. We've done what he said, killed the Wicked Witch of the West, and this golden cap is the proof he said we had to bring. If he's a wizard of his word, he will grant us our wishes. He promised us, didn't he?"

"Promises, promises," Scarecrow mumbled doubtfully to himself as Dorothy was ringing the bell. The gates opened and there stood the same Guardian we had met before, dressed in his green uniform as usual, and with a green moustache, but now it was neatly trimmed. It was strange being in a green place again after all that yellow.

"You've changed," said the Guardian, looking up at the tin man. "You're yellow."

"And you are green," replied Tin Woodman.

"You can't judge people by their colour," said Scarecrow. "It's what goes on in our brains that matters."

"And in our hearts," Tin Woodman added.

"But weren't you going to visit the Wicked Witch of the West?" the Guardian asked, handing us out those same glasses to wear again.

"That's where we've been," Dorothy replied.

"Well, I'm truly amazed she let you go," said the Guardian. "How brave you must have been! It's nice to have you back again."

"And, believe me," Dorothy told him, "we are more than glad to be here. And you are much nicer than when we last saw you. I like your moustache much better, much nicer."

"Thank you," he said. "That is very kind."

I looked at Dorothy and she smiled. I could tell she was only being polite. My sixth sense again.

We were walking up the same street now where we had walked before. Everything was just as bright and sparkling as ever, just as green. And there were the same green sausages in the butcher's window. I licked my lips and Lion licked his! I couldn't resist. I dashed in. No one was looking. No one saw me. Sometimes it is

really useful
to be small.

Lickety-split I snatched the
sausages and was out of there.

Lion and I shared them as we walked along. He
had more than me, but that was only fair – as he was
a bit bigger. Green sausages were the best, I decided,
the best in the whole wide world, even better than
in Kansas, though then I felt a little guilty for liking
anyone's sausages better than Aunt Em's.

The others were walking on, they never even
noticed. We licked our lips clean of course, and then
ran and caught up with them.

"You look happy, Toto," said Dorothy, "which
means you've been naughty. You're wagging your tail
so hard it'll fall off.

"You may not believe this," Dorothy went on,
turning to the Guardian, "but that warty old Wicked
Witch of the West didn't exactly just let us go. We
melted her in water, freezing-cold water."

"Melted her!" the Guardian cried in astonishment. "You melted her, all by yourself?"

"Sort of, you could say that," Dorothy replied, smiling at me. The Guardian was beside himself with joy. He was shouting the news out loud up and down the street, and soon there was a huge crowd following us along, towards the great Palace of Oz in the centre of the city.

"They've done for the Wicked Witch of the West!" the Guardian was shouting it out. "They've melted her, done for her once and for all! She's kicked the bucket, dropped off her perch. The Wicked Witch of the West is a goner!"

The bells began to ring all over the city, and everyone was cheering us, waving to us from windows, showering us with green petals and green roses.

Inside the Palace of Oz, everyone had heard the news and the whole place was a buzz of excitement. "How happy the Great Wizard will be," they cried. To start with we were all a bit bemused by this fuss and bother, but soon enough we began to enjoy it, to bask in the glory of it. Lion and I trotted along, our tails high, waving them proudly. Scarecrow and Tin Woodman and Dorothy waved their hands because they didn't have tails. We were all waving whatever we had to wave, loving every moment of it. We were so happy.

"I shall soon have my heart," said Tin Woodman.

"And I shall soon have my brains," said Scarecrow.

"And I shall soon have courage," said Lion.

"And Toto and I shall soon be home in Kansas with Aunt Em and Uncle Henry," said Dorothy. "Home is . . ."

". . . home," chorused the tin man, the scarecrow and the lion. "And home is best!"

"You're so dog-gone right," I woofed.

We thought we would be shown in at once to see the Great and Terrible Wizard of Oz, but the Guardian said that the wizard always slept in the afternoons and would be pleased to see us in the morning. The Guardian gave us a feast of food, and then showed us to a great bed chamber with a huge wide bed and a roaring log fire from which Scarecrow kept a safe distance.

"Sparks," he said, "aren't good for me." After we had eaten our fill, those of us that ate, we all lay down together on the bed, Scarecrow and Tin Woodman too. They all linked arms, and I lay with my head on Dorothy's lap. We were fast asleep before we knew it. And I dreamed of green sausages and the farmhouse in Kansas and rounding up the cows and chasing rats and rabbits.

Come the morning, the Guardian led us down a long, long corridor to see the Great and Terrible Wizard.

We walked into his throne room, arms linked again, me at Dorothy's heel, all of us happy, all of us full of hope. But the room was strangely silent and empty. There was no one there. Then at last came the voice, his voice. It seemed to come from everywhere, from all around us. "I am Oz, the Great and Terrible," it boomed.

"We know who you are," Dorothy said, looking about her as we all were. "But where are you?"

"I am on my throne, I am invisible. You cannot see me," came the reply. "I hear you have done away with the Wicked Witch of the West."

"We have," replied Dorothy. "And look, I am wearing her magic golden cap to prove it. I melted her with a bucket of water. It was easy, really. And now you must keep your promises, to all of us."

"Promises, promises," came the voice. "Maybe, maybe I will, but I am a bit busy right now. I shall have to think about it. Come back tomorrow. Maybe tomorrow."

"Maybe?" cried Dorothy, stamping her foot angrily. "Now listen here, Mr Wizard, you made promises to us, faithful promises, and you are going to keep them, you hear me?" She was not just angry, she was furious. So I barked, because if Dorothy was furious, I was furious too. Tin Woodman stamped his feet clankily and whirled his axe about his head, and Scarecrow

too was mad with anger, shaking himself so hard that his straw began to fall out. And Lion roared. He let out a roar that shook the chandeliers and rattled the windows. He was standing right beside me.

I hadn't been expecting a roar like that. The shock of it made me jump half out of my skin. I turned and bolted. I was so frightened I ran smack right into a silk screen and sent it crashing to the ground.

And, to our complete astonishment, we saw standing there, where the silk screen had been, a little old man, rather bald, with wispy hair, in a raggedy tweed suit, wearing a monocle and leaning on a cane. Dorothy cried out in her surprise, I barked, the lion roared, Tin Woodman raised his axe again, and Scarecrow was waving his arms and rustling his straw as he always did when he was agitated. No one said a word.

"You are the Wizard of Oz?" Dorothy breathed at last.

"Well, kind of," the old man replied. "Sort of, I guess. You could say that."

CHAPTER FOURTEEN

The Really Confusing Wizard of Oz

*A*s you can imagine, little puppies, after such a
shock it took quite a while for all of us to calm
down. Dorothy was the first to find her voice. "Who
are you?" she said. "And where is the Wizard of Oz?"

"Oh dear," replied the old man, shaking his head
sadly. "Oh dear, oh dear. I'm ashamed to have to say
that you are looking at him. I am the Great and Terrible
Wizard of Oz."

"But you looked like a sort of huge Humpty

Dumpty," said Dorothy.

"Then a beautiful lady," said Tin Woodman.

"Then a hideous beast a bit like a horrible, spidery rhino with cruel claws," said Lion. "Scared me rigid, you did."

"And you were a great ball of fire too," said Scarecrow. "I remember you were, because I don't like fire. I don't like fire at all."

"They are right," said Dorothy. "You were all these things, one after the other. It was very confusing!"

"Oh, I do apologise," the old man cried, wringing his hands. "It was all nothing but make-believe. I am nothing but a humbug, a low-down trickster, a miserable fraudster."

"So you are not a great wizard at all," Dorothy said.

He put his finger to his lips. "Shhh," he whispered. "No one else must know. If I am found out, I am done for. Everyone in the Emerald City will hate me. And I can't bear being hated. I like to be liked and loved, to be admired. Doesn't everyone? Don't blame me too harshly, and please, please don't tell them."

"But," said Tin Woodman, "if you are not a wizard, you can't give me a heart, can you?"

"And you can't give me brains," said Scarecrow.

"And who else will give me courage?" said Lion.

"And, if you don't mind my asking, how will Toto and I get ourselves back to Kansas without the magic of the Wizard of Oz? You promised us, promised all of us. And we went and got rid of the Wicked Witch of the West like you said. It's not fair, it's not right and it's not fair."

"You are right, Dorothy," said the old man, "but believe me I didn't do it on purpose. One thing just seemed to lead to another. I couldn't help myself. I mean, I didn't want to be here at all in the first place."

"Neither did I, nor Toto, nor any of us," Dorothy told him. "We want to go home, but we don't know where home is, nor how to get there even if we did. I mean, we know our farmhouse is in the land of the Munchkins, because that's where we landed after the twister that sucked us up into the air." And then Dorothy told the old man all that had happened to us since we landed, our meeting with Scarecrow and Tin Woodman, Lion, and all our adventures together. It took a while and was quite boring, because we knew the story already, of course.

"And we never saw Aunt Em and Uncle Henry ever again, and now we never shall." And Dorothy cried then, sobbing her heart out.

"Don't cry, my dear," said the old man. He looked thoughtful. "Maybe there's a way I can still help you, help you all. 'Where there's a will, there's a way,' that's what I say."

"That's what my Aunt Em used to say too," Dorothy said, brightening a little as Tin Woodman wiped away her tears.

Scarecrow was scratching his head.

"I don't understand. Well, I wouldn't, would I? No brains, you see. But how come, if you're not a real and proper wizard, you could change yourself just like that, be a baldy old egghead one moment, then a lovely lady, then that nasty beast, then a great ball of fire? I don't understand."

"It's a fair question, Scarecrow, that needs an honest answer. Perhaps I should tell you my story. I think I owe you some explanation after all the trouble I have been to you," said the old man, who always spoke very politely. "Follow me," he went on, "and I will show you everything, tell you everything."

We followed him through a curtain behind the throne and there on the floor lay the great pearly-white head we had last seen on the throne. "You see that wire up there above your head?" he said. "I just clip that Humpty Dumpty head, as you call it, on to the wire and hoist it up. Then I can pull

the strings to make the mouth open and shut. It's just a kind of puppet head, all made of wire and papier-mâché. That's all it is. And when I speak I can change my voice, become a man or woman or fearsome beast, and I can throw it too, make it seem as if it sounds very near or far away. You see, I am a ventriloquist and an actor, a showman."

He gave Dorothy a chair. "Sit down, my dear," he said. "This will take some time.

"I play many parts," he went on. "The young lady, the beautiful one, was me in a mask and a long green dress, and of course with a different voice; the nasty, spidery beast with the rhino's head – that was me too. There's the head on the chair over there." Somehow it did not look at all frightening on the chair. "Look at all my costumes hanging up, dozens of them, I made them all myself. And the great ball of fire? My chef-d'oeuvre, my masterpiece! It was simply a gigantic ball of cotton, soaked in oil and set on fire, then I just speak in a fiery sort of a voice. It's easy when you know how.

If there is one thing I have learnt in all my days as a travelling showman, it is that if I play my part well, people will always believe in who I am, in what I want them to believe; and this is mostly because they wish to believe what they want to believe."

"I only half understood that," said Scarecrow, scratching his head, "and I am not sure which half either."

"Do you come from these parts?" asked Tin Woodman.

"Oh no, not at all," the old man replied. "Do I look green or blue or yellow? No, I come from Omaha, which is—"

"In America!" cried Dorothy. "Where Kansas is, where we come from! How did you get here? Were you carried up by a twister like we were?"

"Well almost, you might say," he replied. "I travel to country fairs, rodeos and the like, doing quite well too. But I had taken my show on the road for years and years, and was becoming tired of it all. Then one day, I happened to be travelling along the road to my next country fair, when I saw an air-balloon flying overhead. I'd never seen one before. It landed at the very same country fair I was going to. I could not imagine anything more wonderful than to go up in such a balloon, to see the world from way up there. I had to pay to go up in it that first time, but it was worth it. It changed my whole life. When I came down, I at once got a job as a balloonist's assistant, then a year or two later as a real balloonist. There's no better job in the world, believe you me. You're up there with the birds, in your basket hanging from the balloon, and flying over mountains and rivers and meadows.

"But then one day it all went a bit wrong. I was up there alone, when the wind got up and the balloon started turning, whirling round and round, and soon the ropes that held the basket to the balloon became twisted. Up I went, up and up through the clouds, higher and higher, so high it was difficult to breathe, and I fell fast asleep. When I woke, I found myself being carried through the streets of a green city, and the people were green too. Everything and everyone was green. I was the only one who wasn't. So to them I was a wonder of the world.

"And maybe because I had come down magically from the sky – from nowhere, it seemed to them – they thought I must be some kind of a wizard, with magical powers, and they treated me with such respect and honour, and I liked that. 'What's your name?' they asked me. 'Oz,' I told them, which was sort of true. 'The Great Ozzy Mandias' had been my stage name, my show business name back in Omaha. So they called me the Wizard of Oz, set me up in a great palace, built it especially for me.

"They were so good and kind to me, these people, as they have been ever since. I couldn't let them down, could I? I couldn't tell them that I was just an ordinary travelling showman from Omaha who had lost his way in a hot-air balloon, could I? So I pretended to be what they wanted me to be. I used all the tricks I had learnt in show business, all my skills as a ventriloquist, hid behind my masks and my costumes and my voices, and I promised I would use all my powers, the powers they believed I had, to protect them from the Wicked Witch of the East and her horrible warty sister, the Wicked Witch of the West — she was the worst of all. They lived in fear and trembling of her especially, because she lived closer — which is why I tricked you into getting rid of her, which you did most successfully, surprisingly successfully. The real truth is that you, Dorothy — with the power of your red shoes, and the golden cap you are wearing, and the kiss from the Good Witch of the North I can see on your forehead — you are much more of a wizard than I am. I'm afraid I am just a selfish, vain and foolish old man who made you rash promises that I cannot keep."

He hung his head. "I am so sorry. I have no magic to offer you. I cannot get you home."

At this dreadful news, I thought Dorothy must lose heart, but she was up on her feet and wagging her finger at him – she reminded me greatly of Aunt Em when she did this!

"You are a bad man," she told him, "a very bad man."

The old man smiled sadly. "You are right, I suppose, but, as you can see now, I am an even worse wizard, and I truly hate myself for being such a humbug. But don't give up on me yet. I'm not all bad. As I said, maybe there is a way I can still put things right. You will all like me if I can, won't you? I do so like to be liked. Let me think about it overnight. Meanwhile you will be my honoured guests in the palace. Everyone will make sure you are warm and comfortable as can be, and you will have all you want to eat. But, whatever you do, please don't tell anyone the truth about me. They would be so disappointed in me for being a humbug, if I turn out not to be the Great Wizard of Oz."

So we said goodnight to the Wizard of Oz – who wasn't a wizard at all, of course. All of us decided we liked him despite this, and all of us hoped that somehow, some way, he could make our wishes come true. I liked him because he tickled the top of my head in just the right place, and because he smelt of old clothes and pipe tobacco, just like Uncle Henry back home.

Dorothy said, as we all lay down on our great wide bed that night, that we should look out of the window, choose a star and make a last wish before we went to sleep, and she told us we should wish the best, not just for each of ourselves, but more for each other, because we were all the best of friends. I nudged her cheek with my cold, cold nose just to remind her that I was her best friend, not the others. But I think she was fast asleep already.

CHAPTER FIFTEEN

—◆—

The Wizardest
Balloonist
There Ever Was

*O*ne... two... three... four... five... six little
puppies asleep. Just you left awake, Tiny Toto.
You're my best listener, you always are. Come up here
and snuggle a little closer. I can whisper then, so I
won't wake your brothers and sisters up. Easy does it,
you're treading all over them, getting your own back,
I guess? Comfy now? Lay your head right there, just
like I used to with Dorothy. Still do, come to that.
Now, Tiny Toto, where was I? Oh yes, here we go.

After the most sumptuous breakfast the next morning – Lion had twenty green sausages, and I had six, which was quite enough for me – the Guardian with the green moustache came to fetch us. Still licking our lips, Lion and I padded along the corridor after the others towards the great throne room. The Guardian knocked on the door. "I'm warning you," he whispered, "he's feeling a bit ferocious this morning, as ferocious as any lion."

"Enter," came the reply, but strangely in a voice we all knew very well. It was Lion speaking, and he was right next to us. We looked at him, amazed.

"Enter," came the voice again, a loud deep roar of a voice, a lion's voice, but Lion's lips weren't moving. He was shrugging his shoulders.

"Not me," he whispered, terrified. "I never said anything. Honest."

Well, we all knew that Lion never told a lie. "I don't like this," he said, backing away from the door. "It's too weird. I don't like weird. And it's scary too, I mean hearing your own voice when you're not saying anything. That's scary. I'm not going in there."

Dorothy put a comforting arm round his neck and ruffled his mane. "You'll be all right," she said.

"If you say so," said Lion, "if you say so." But he didn't sound at all convinced.

In we went, and there was a lion sitting on the throne, and not just any old lion, but just like our lion, and he was roaring at us. "Come along in," he was roaring. "I may roar, but I won't bite." He was beckoning us in with his paw. "Guardian, my friends and I have a lot to talk about. We do not wish to be disturbed."

"Your wish is my command, oh Great and Terrible Wizard," said the Guardian with the green moustache, bowing low and walking backwards out of the throne room. The lion on the throne waited till the door closed, and then stood up, taking off his head at once. The old man's face was wreathed in smiles, his eyes twinkling merrily.

"Well, what do you think?" he said, coming down the steps towards us, carrying his head with him. "I stayed up all night making the costume, and practising my lion talk. How did I do, Lion?"

"Amazing," said Lion. "But I do wish you wouldn't roar quite so loud. Frightens me to death." The old man had taken off all his lion costume by now. He came over and stroked the top of my head.

"I had a dog like you once, Toto," he said, "just like you. My best friend in the world he was. I left him behind when I went up in the balloon that day – he never liked flying – and I never saw him again. Diddledeedoo, I called him. I still miss him every day."

"Just like I miss home, and Aunt Em and Uncle Henry," said Dorothy. "Now I'm sorry about you, and your Diddledeedoo dog, I really am, but my friends and I, we want some answers. We thank you most kindly for your hospitality – the green sausages were excellent – but you did say you would try to work something out for us. You promised."

"Yes, you promised," we all said, me too in my own barking way.

The old man nodded, but said nothing. Then he put his hands behind his back and began walking up and down in front of us. "You're right. I promised," he began. "All night while I was making my lion costume I was thinking. You know now that I have no magic powers, that I am simply Mr Ozzy Mandias, showman extraordinaire maybe, but not the Wizard of Oz. When you play many parts, as actors like me do, you have to understand not just about how people look and speak and feel, but about how people are, why they do what they do. Dorothy told me yesterday everything that has happened to you in all your adventures and what good friends you all are. She told it all so well, that I feel as if I have known you, each of you, for ever."

He stopped in front of Scarecrow and looked up at him. "Dear Scarecrow," he said, "you think you want brains in that straw head of yours, because you think you are stupid. You want to be wise. To be wise you have to work things out, to ask questions, to think for yourself. You do all these things. I have heard of all you have done and said. So you are wise already, dear Scarecrow. You have all the brains you need. All you have to do is believe in yourself. You are perfect just as you are, a fine and wise Scarecrow. You do not need some wizard or magic to make you so."

He came to Tin Woodman next. "And, dear Tin Woodman, you say you need a heart. Well, I have thought long and hard about you. I could indeed cut a hole in your tin chest and make you a pretty heart out of silk, and stuff it in you and solder you together again What clumsy and pointless magic that would be.

The thing you need to know, dear Tin Woodman, is that you don't need a silken heart or any other kind of heart. I have heard of all you have done, so I know you have one already, a good and kind heart. Look around you. Think about it. You have friends you love, and they love you. Could they love a heartless person? Why do you think you are moved so easily to tears, why do you cry so much?" He knocked on the tin man's chest. "All you have to do, dear Tin Woodman, is believe that you already have a heart. Believe me, you have all the heart you need. But you don't have to believe me. Ask your friends, they will tell you."

And we did, all of us in our own way. Woofing is my way.

"As for you, dear Lion," he went on, stroking Lion's golden mane, "who says he has no courage; well, excuse me, but you really should know yourself better. Yes, you are fearful sometimes, but you conquer your fear. And this is true courage. A brave lion who knows no fear is not brave at all. What do you want, some magic green medicine I could pour down your throat

and fill you up with courage? You don't need it. I have heard of all the brave things you have done, so I know you already have all the courage you need to be a king of all beasts, king of the jungle."

"Really?" said the lion. "Are you quite sure?"

"Quite sure," replied the old man.

"But what about me and Toto?" Dorothy asked. "How are we ever going to get back to Kansas?"

"Well, this is a little more difficult, I'm afraid," he began, "but in a way, it was your little Toto here who gave me the idea that I might be able to help." I was trying to work out what I had done, but could not think of anything. "You see," said the old man, "I have been here many years, and I should like to go home myself."

"Home is home," said Dorothy quietly, "and home is best."

"Undeniable," said the old man.

"Woof," I woofed.

"I've been happy enough here in the Emerald City," the old man said. "The people are kind, I have all I need; but it isn't easy every day to pretend to be someone you are not. And seeing Toto reminded me of my dear little Diddledeedoo back home in Omaha, and how dreadfully I miss him. And, if I'm honest, I'm a bit fed up with these spells and witches and all this magic stuff. So I was thinking that sometimes the best ideas are the upside-down ideas, don't you think? I was thinking last night: 'What comes down must go up.' Upside-down thinking, you see. My balloon and I came down here in the Emerald City, so maybe it could go up again, with us in it. They keep the balloon in the Wizard of Oz Museum in the city. They repainted it after I arrived here, fixed it up. It's all in perfect working order. We could leave today, if we wanted to, just take it out into the square, light a fire under the balloon, fill it with hot air and away we go."

"You mean we could go home today?" cried Dorothy, dancing around the room in her red shoes. "Do you hear that, Toto? Do you hear that?" Well, I'd heard it, of course, but I could see the look on Tin Woodman's face, see the tears rolling down his cheeks, I could see Lion holding his paws up to his face and sobbing, and Scarecrow trying to comfort them both.

Then Dorothy noticed too, and ran over to them.

"Oh, please don't be sad," she cried. "You could come with us to Kansas. I'm sure Aunt Em and Uncle Henry would like you to come with us, wouldn't they, Toto?" Now that was a grand idea, I thought, so I told them so, I barked them so. We would all of us be together for ever!

But Scarecrow was shaking his head. "No," he said. "That's very kind of you, Dorothy, but I would rather go home to the land of the Munchkins where I come from. I liked it there. It's home for me."

"And I will go back to the land of the yellow Winkies," said Tin Woodman. "After all, they saved my life and painted me yellow so now I don't rust even when I cry. And, anyway, I like being yellow as the sun like them. They will look after me and I will look after them. They told me to come back if ever I wanted to. I've always wanted a place to belong. It'll be home for me."

"And I will stay here, Dorothy," said Lion, "in this place where I found my courage, where I became who

I am, thanks to the Great and Terrible Wizard of Oz, or Mr Ozzy Mandias, whichever you are. I will be the only golden creature that lives here. I can hunt in the fields and forests round about. Why would I ever want to live anywhere else? It'll be home for me."

"Better than that, Lion, my friend," said the old man excitedly, "when we leave I shall be able to tell them that the king of beasts himself will be looking after them instead of me."

"And can I have green sausages every day?" the Lion asked.

"You'll be king," replied the old man, "you will be able to have everything you want!"

"That'll do then," said Lion. "I'm happy."

And all the people were happy too when they heard Lion would be staying on instead of the wizard – he'd been shut away in the palace all this time anyway, they hadn't seen much of him.

But it wouldn't be true to say that Scarecrow and Tin Woodman and Lion were happy when the balloon was full of hot air and we were ready to leave. There were a lot of tears – in fact, not from me or Scarecrow or Lion, because none of us could cry, but from Dorothy. Dorothy can cry for Kansas! And she did. And so did all the people too, and Tin Woodman of course.

The balloon was tugging at its ropes. The time came for hurried goodbyes. I got a prickly cuddle from Scarecrow, a clanking cuddle from Tin Woodman, and a huge lion hug from Lion, and a mouthful of mane too!

Dorothy stood up on tiptoe and kissed Tin Woodman on his forehead tenderly. "I'm leaving you the kiss the Good Witch of the North gave me. It protected me and it will protect you. Goodbye, dear friend." To Scarecrow, she said, "I'm giving you my magic red shoes. They won't fit, but that doesn't matter. Keep them always, so you won't forget us, Toto and me, and all our wonderful adventures together. I hope they will protect you as they have protected me. Goodbye, dear friend." Then she turned to Lion and put the golden cap on his head. "If ever you need any help from those Winged Monkeys, put this on and wish. Remember you have only three wishes, so don't waste any. They will do as you command. Goodbye, dear friend."

Then to all of them, she said, "You make me think that friendship and kindness are the most important things in all the world."

They all nodded, but were too tearful to speak. Then the old man, Dorothy and I climbed inside the basket. Dorothy had her own basket still, of course, the one over her arm that she had carried all the time wherever she went, with Uncle Henry's hat still inside it. She was holding me close and I could see her eyes were filling with tears again.

"Goodbye, dear friends," she cried. "Be happy. I shall think of you often, dream of you every night. We will meet again in our dreams. We will always be the best of friends."

As the balloon rose slowly into the air, Dorothy was waving, the old man too. And everyone down there below us on the ground was waving back. The Guardian with the green moustache was saluting us, the tears running down his face. Up and up we rose,

leaving the Emerald City sparkling below us. We could see the yellow brick road winding its way through the green of the countryside, the road we knew so well, and then we were lost in the clouds.

"Excuse me, Ozzy, if I may call you that," Dorothy said, after a while, "I think we might have one small problem. We are up here, and that is fine, but how do we know which way to go? How do we find our way back to Kansas?"

"I suppose we go wherever the wind takes us," said the old man. "That's how I got here, after all. Isn't that what happens in life, Dorothy? It's what happens in balloons just the same. And don't you worry, I'm just about the wizardest balloonist there ever was. I'll get you back to Kansas, you'll see." He looked down at me and smiled. I believed him. But I was not enjoying this at all. I had discovered, after looking over the side for too long, that I didn't have a head for heights.

I guess you can't exactly get seasick in a balloon, but I reckon that's what being seasick feels like. *Creep into a corner of the basket, curl up and go to sleep*, I told myself. *Pretend it isn't happening; no nightmare could be as bad as this*. Dorothy was so excited and she wouldn't come and lie down with me and cuddle me no matter how much I whined and I whimpered for her. So I sulked there on my own and pretty soon I was asleep. Sulking often helps me go to sleep, I find.

I woke up with a walloping bump and a crash. "Hang on," the old man was shouting. But I couldn't hang on. Fortunately, Dorothy grabbed me just in time, otherwise I would have been thrown out of the basket altogether as it toppled over. "You'd better get out," the old man was telling us, "this balloon is dragging along pretty fast. I reckon she wants to take off again at any moment. Out you jump, Dorothy!" So Dorothy jumped, clinging on to me as tightly as she could. We rolled over and over and over. Then we were lying there on our backs, all the breath bumped out of us, watching the balloon rising into the air above us, the old man waving.

"I hope you find your Diddledeedoo!" Dorothy was shouting up at him.

"And I hope you find your home!" cried the old man. "I reckon this is Kansas, by the look of it. Plenty of tumbleweed about. Trouble with Kansas is it's mighty big."

"We'll find it soon enough," Dorothy cried, waving back.

And so we did too. Dorothy asked about, hitched a ride here and a ride there. Everyone was so friendly, just as friendly as anyone we had met in the Land of Oz. And the food was a whole lot better. These folk understood what a dog likes to eat.

And then, after a week or so, we found ourselves walking up the track towards home, towards the farmhouse, which looked just about the same, but newer – the old one had blown away, if you remember. The cows were out there grazing away in the fields, the

hens were all clucking about the yard, and the wind was blowing wild all across the plains, and there was plenty of tumbleweed rolling about and chasing itself.

We were home sure enough! And there was Uncle Henry ploughing a field and Aunt Em hanging up the washing on the line. They both saw us at about the same time. At first they couldn't believe their eyes, then they came running as fast as their legs could carry them.

"Dorothy! Toto! Where have you been?" Aunt Em cried. So Dorothy told them, and went on telling them and telling them, but they wouldn't believe her, and they still don't believe her now, all these years later. People folk are like that, my little puppies. Haven't got no imagination, you see, that's their problem.

Anyways, Dorothy and I got home safe and sound, and boy were they glad to see us! Aunt Em gave us a good scolding for going off like we had and scaring the living daylights out of her. And Uncle Henry was happy, because he'd got his hat back.

None of it would have happened, of course, if the twister hadn't come and blowed away his hat. And none of it would have happened if I hadn't chased after it and brought it home. And that's the dog-gone truth!

EPILOGUE

Well, That's
My Story Done

"*Well, that's my story done.*"

That was how Papa Toto would always end his tale.

All the other little puppies were snoozing away, lost in their own dreams.

"*You asleep too, Tiny Toto?*" *Papa Toto said.* "*That's good. I'm fairly tired out myself with all this storytelling. Still, it did its job, got you lot to go to sleep. So now I'm going to have a bit of a sleep myself. Think I deserve it.*"

But I wasn't asleep, not really. I just had my eyes closed, that's all. I never once went to sleep during Papa Toto's tale, which is why I know it so well, I guess. I only ever went to sleep when he did, my head resting on his heart, so I could feel us breathing together.

I always loved that.